PENELOPE'S MAN

In this new romance John Erskine taps prodigally the springs of pagan laughter. It is that rare phenomenon, an uproarious story that yet retains its subtlety, and its sharp, unstrained characterizations. Odysseus is its hero, but in recounting his adventures Dr. Erskine exercises the same privilege used by Homer himself, of reinterpreting borrowed material for the needs and moods of his own generation. He acknowledges indebtedness to Hesiod, to the Greek Dramatists, to Apollonius of Rhodes. But learning is lost in a grin; and the Trojan heroes become men of like manner with ourselves.

After the siege of Troy Odysseus was heartsick for home and for his wife Penelope; the years of wandering, with their narrow escapes from the wiles of Circe, Calypso, the Sirens and other dangerous ladies were a sore trial to the hero, says Homer. Not at all, says Erskine; on the contrary he enjoyed it, and in fact deliberately steered his course so as not to miss any of the charmers.

We get some startling new data upon the characters of Odysseus and his noble band, and witness not a few encounters which lose something in the telling when the wanderer finally describes them to his wife. As for the ladies themselves, including Penelope—

But it would be unchivalrous to give away any more.

PENELOPE'S MAN

THE HOMING INSTINCT

BY

JOHN ERSKINE

END PAPERS BY
D. PUTNAM BRINLEY

INDIANAPOLIS
THE BOBBS-MERRILL COMPANY
PUBLISHERS

PRESS OF
BRAUNWORTH & CO., INC.
BOOK MANUFACTURERS
BROOKLYN, N. Y.

NOTE

The reader will recognize my debt for some of these fancies to Hesiod, to the Greek Dramatists, to the *Argonautica* of Apollonius Rhodius, and to familiar modern works of interpretation and criticism, such as *Studies in the Odyssey*, by J. A. K. Thomson, and *The Golden Bough*, by J. G. Frazer.

J. E.

CONTENTS

PART ONE

THE WOODEN HORSE

PENELOPE'S MAN

PART ONE

THE WOODEN HORSE

ODYSSEUS was ten years getting home from Troy.
Homer made a hero out of him, the type of those
who, though tossed about by waves of ocean or of
fate, are resourceful and patient. Homer was his
best friend.

Oddly enough, Odysseus was no great admirer
of Helen. It may have been this peculiarity which
caused her to speak of him always with respect.
Unless you read carefully, you get the impression
that he was one of her many suitors, pledged with
them to stand by the lucky man who won her;
therefore he went to Troy with the rest, and
through his cleverness—the wooden horse, and all

[11]

that—enabled the Greeks to catch the beautiful
but naughty woman, and make her live with her
husband again. A competent citizen, with an eye
to the interests of the community.

The facts are otherwise. He was only tech-
nically a suitor, not being in love with that particular lady, and though he did swear to help
Menelaos if any one ran off with her, yet when the
clearly foreseen accident occurred, he tried to back
out. Not that he was a coward, but he had no stake
in that war. When the city was tottering and the
Greeks were exhausted, both sides having had
enough, he did invent that absurd wooden machine,
but a woman had a hand in the affair, the very
woman, Helen herself.

Indeed, most of his exploits involve women.
Some of them are called goddesses, but it comes to
the same thing. He had a gift for narrative, and
could bestow romance upon the bleakest episode.
So many women, in fact, that Samuel Butler insisted the *Odyssey* must have been composed by a
female partial to her sex, an aggressive feminist.
When you look into it, you don't know whether to

call the hero "much wandering, much tossed about," or "much mothered." If these women hadn't taken him in, furnished him with bed and board and passed him along, he never would have got home.

It's time his doings were reported from their point of view. The wooden-horse affair, to begin with.

The Greeks were holding a council in the evening, active combat having ceased at supper-time.

Agamemnon summed up his opinion in a few vigorous words. "As I see it, we've been here ten years, and we're getting nowhere. Five years ago the prospect was bright. The Trojans came out almost every day, and Achilles would cut them down. The mortality exceeded the birth-rate, and time was a factor on our side. After Achilles died, we lost ground, but since his efficient son joined us and took his place, the favorable ratio has been restored, or would be if the Trojans hadn't adopted their present despicable tactics. They now decline to come out and be killed. This campaign has become static."

He sat down, and many in the circle commented privately on his lucid style and his realistic turn of thought. Odysseus stood up and cleared his throat.

"Though I agree with the previous speaker as to our condition at the moment, I see no reason why our strategy should remain paralyzed."

"I didn't say our strategy is paralyzed," interrupted Agamemnon, "I said the campaign is static. You don't, by any chance, imply criticism of my command?"

"I imply nothing. I was about to contribute an idea. If the Trojans won't come out, we'll have to go in."

He sat down, and many in the circle reflected how simple the problems of life are, when a real mind gets to work on them. But Agamemnon was not impressed.

"If I get your idea," he said, "we're to knock on the gate and ask them to open up. I move that Odysseus be elected a committee of one to call on the Trojans."

The King of Ithaca declined to be rebuked.

[14]

"My plan contemplated a certain elaboration which would involve the whole army. If I'm not taking up too much of this assembly's valuable time?"

Agamemnon grunted. "Go on, we've nothing else to do."

"Well, then, why not build an immense effigy of wood, a figure suitable for worship in a temple, but hollow, so that a number of us can hide inside? Leave it where it will attract the attention of the Trojans, who will then welcome it as the symbol of a god come to aid them."

"And what happens next?" said Agamemnon.

"They'll take it into the city, of course, and during the night those of us concealed within will creep out, unlock the gates and admit the others."

The council couldn't resist a round of applause—all except Agamemnon.

"This god or idol we're to make—you didn't say what the thing is to look like."

"A horse," said Odysseus. "Since it's to be found on the shore, they will think it's a gift from the sea, one of Poseidon's horses."

Agamemnon laughed, not in a complimentary tone.

"This proposal strikes me as ridiculous. Even if we could build such a contrivance with enough resemblance to the animal to deceive the near-sighted, and even if the Trojans should want the monster in their town, how could they move it? With a number of us inside, too!"

Odysseus was ready for him.

"Before burdening you with this suggestion, I talked it over with the ship's carpenter. He thinks he could make a passable horse, in fact, a rather artistic representation. You've all noticed the life-like emblem on the prow of my boat—we've only to repeat it on a larger scale. As for moving it, we'll provide rollers."

"Do you think I'd ask any friend," said Agamemnon, "to go to his death in that crazy trap? The Trojans would probably burn it as a thank-offering—that is, if we had gone home. Unless we go, you couldn't build a horse fascinating enough to lure them out. And besides, we don't know what sort of guard they keep in Troy—even if the plan worked, the men in the horse wouldn't know how to let in the rest of the army."

The council thought it over, and the wooden horse began to look a bit impracticable.

"Unless," continued the chief, "some reckless idiot here volunteers to pay a call on the city, as I suggested a moment ago, and ask them just what their internal arrangements are."

The assembly laughed, seizing the excuse of his sarcasm to hide their general aversion to spy duty. Odysseus was stung; he wasn't accustomed to public ignominy.

"If my plan is adopted, *I'll* volunteer! I'm no more eager than the rest of you to die, but it's this or nothing. If you had any ideas yourself, Agamemnon, your smartish talk would be more appropriate. But now I make you a fair offer—if this assembly will vote to build the wooden horse and try out my plan, I'll enter Troy to-night and learn how to open the gates!"

While the votes were being counted, he rather hoped they would reject his plan. "Perhaps I was hasty," he said, "in promising to go to-night."

One or two of his companions snickered.

"There isn't time to get well started before dark. But to-morrow evening."

"Don't hurry yourself," said Agamemnon. "If I know the ship's carpenter, the horse won't be ready."

The next evening Odysseus was in Troy, talking with Helen.

He had gone around and entered by the eastern gate, disguised as one of the neutral merchants who at the moment were doing a heavy trade with the wealthier families among the besieged, buying superfluous rugs and objects of art in exchange for food. He wore a shabby coat, he had cut off his flowing hair, he had reduced his splendid beard to a state suggesting that he hadn't been shaved for a week. In short, he looked like a rug merchant, of the poorer and more persistent sort. The one weapon he carried, a sharp knife, was gracefully disposed under his left arm, where it wouldn't show.

He had accumulated several articles of value, and had got rid of all the food Agamemnon had

[18]

been willing to invest, but as yet he had learned nothing about the city gates. Discouraged, he sat down on the steps of the nearest porch. It was a fine house, but he didn't care. He wished he had eaten some of the good things now represented by the heavy bundle of rugs at his feet. Hunger told on him more than danger.

A very beautiful girl stuck her head out the door.

"You'll have to move on, or I'll call the janitor."

"Young woman, the janitor isn't necessary. If you could provide me with a modest sandwich or two, as any wayfarer has the right to expect of a well-mannered household——"

"Our manners are as they should be, but we have no sandwiches. You move on!"

She was quite outside the door, menacing but altogether charming. Odysseus appraised her figure with the eye of a connoisseur. In two or three years, when she should be a bit more mature——

"You move on, I say! I don't like your looks at all!"

[19]

Odysseus adjusted the rugs and leaned against them, ready for intimate conversation.

"Young woman, I suspect this house does not belong to you. If you'll ask the true owner to step out here, I'd like a word with him. Or, as the case may be, with her."

The girl's eyes narrowed.

"You suspect it doesn't belong to me, do you? Do you know what I suspect? I suspect you're a spy. You'd better move on before I call the police. The last one they caught didn't enjoy himself."

"Didn't he?" Odysseus was trying to keep his voice easy and nonchalant. "Of course he wouldn't. They killed him, naturally."

"It came to that, in the end." She implied something very bad.

"Served him right! We can't have spies coming in here." His throat was a little dry.

"I suppose not," said the girl, softening, "but I don't see why we must be so cruel."

"Oh, was it cruel?"

"Was it! I didn't see it done myself. They stuck a sharp stake up through him, and planted it

in the ground. They say his wrigglings were unusually protracted."

Odysseus was very angry.

"That's what you'd expect of barbarians! We
cut throats when it's necessary, but we don't
torture!"

Her eyes narrowed again, and she backed toward
the door.

"We don't, don't we? Who's 'we'?"

"I come from a remote people, toward the East,"
said Odysseus. "If I say it myself, a civilized people, given to the arts rather than to war."

"Are you all beggars?"

He was thinking up a disarming answer, when
a strong rough-looking man, a servant probably,
pushed out of the house behind the girl.

"What's going on here, Adraste?"

"It's a Greek spy, just dropping in for a little
talk with the owner of the house. And before he
betrays the city, he'd like a sandwich."

The man laughed and walked over toward
Odysseus.

"Where do you come from?"

"From the East. As the young woman knows perfectly, I'm a rug dealer. Don't you folks let an innocent traveler rest a moment on the doorstep? She's been trying to scare me out of it."

The man looked him over.

"You talk like a Greek," he said, "but the evil state of your person suggests descent from rug dealers. If you are now sufficiently rested, would you mind getting off our porch? You are no ornament."

Odysseus rose slowly, as he had seen beggars do.

"My Greek accent," he said, "I picked up in that country on business trips before the war. They are in the wrong now, of course; if I weren't loyal to Troy, I wouldn't be here at this minute. But your inhospitality compels me to say that no Greek ever treated me so badly. You might learn from them."

"From who? Those fellows who've been trying for ten years to get in here? Agamemnon's an ass."

"There's something in that," said Odysseus. "He's overrated."

"And Menelaos is worse, by all accounts."

"Oh, you can't trust gossip. Menelaos has his points."

The man sat down on the step beside him, and Odysseus decided to stay a while longer. The girl leaned against the door, listening.

"When you used to visit Greece, before the war, did you ever see those two?"

"Often. We were——"

He was about to add "old friends," but remembered just in time.

"Well, there may be something to them, but what I'd like to know is, why that rascal Odysseus attacked us. He must have a pretty mean streak in him."

"On the contrary," said Odysseus. "It has often occurred to me that he has more brains than all his allies put together. Certainly a gifted man, and one of the few who take part in this war for high-minded reasons. The motives of the others are, I understand, selfish."

"I see," said the man, "you don't know much about them, after all. Odysseus is nothing but a

[23]

chatterer. Talks all the time. Never did a brave thing in his life."

"Again I disagree," said Odysseus. "He has great abilities. What we need is some one like him on the Trojan side."

"All right—you can have his job."

The man moved a little closer to Odysseus, and took hold of his wrist. "Adraste, you may call the police. You guessed right—this fellow's a spy!"

Odysseus thought fast.

"Call the whole force, whenever you like." He fancied his tone sounded mildly amused. When the man looked the other way, he would get out the hidden knife.

"We shan't need the whole force—one or two will be enough, Adraste."

The girl departed down the street, in no unseemly haste. Odysseus watched her for a moment. When he gave his attention again to his captor, he was shocked to see his knife in the fellow's hand. The man was disgustingly pleased with himself.

"Now we'll just sit here quietly," he said, "until they come to take you."

"Rest is what I need," said Odysseus, "but if I'm not mistaken, you have helped yourself to my property. That knife is of no intrinsic value, but it has sentimental associations. My father, an old man, gave it to me when I went in business. I carry it for his sake."

The man handled the weapon with respect, testing the point and running his thumb along the blade.

"Your sentiment," he said, "has quite an edge on it."

Odysseus dropped the subject. He wondered whether it would be worth while to try bribery.

"Have you noticed my rugs? There are several in that bundle which money couldn't buy. Let me show you."

He stooped down to unroll them, but the man wasn't interested. In fact he laid the point of the knife very neatly against Odysseus' ribs.

"Sit up straight there! We'll examine your plunder later. The owners have probably sent in descriptions of it already."

"I didn't steal it!" said Odysseus.

"My mistake! No doubt they made you a present of it."

They watched each other through another silence.

"By the way," said Odysseus, "this is a very nice house you have."

"We'll always remember that it had your approval," said the fellow.

"It's yours, of course?"

"In the same sense as the city's yours. You're a captive, and I'm a slave."

Odysseus saw a line to develop.

"I didn't realize we were in the same boat. From your appearance I thought——"

"Yes you did!" sneered the man.

"I suppose," said Odysseus, "you'd be glad to run away, if you had a good chance and a little aid?"

"You suppose wrong. I've a good berth."

A second later he wished he had drawn Odysseus out.

"Supposing I did want to run, what then?"

His tone was too crafty.

[26]

"Oh, nothing," said Odysseus. "I was just feeling sorry for you."

The man grunted. A long minute went by.

"Who does own the house, if you don't?"

"I like your nerve—as though you didn't know!"

"My word of honor, I don't!"

"You must be one of those Greek orators," said the man. "What's the use of lying when I can see through you?"

Odysseus put on his most offended dignity.

"When I report your conduct to the Court," he began, "the Trojan judges, for whom I have the greatest respect, will——"

"They'll never lay eyes on you. We dispose of spies automatically."

They watched each other again.

"That charming young woman," said Odysseus, "whose name I didn't catch, must have gone for a long walk. Or perhaps the police force is occupied elsewhere this evening?"

The man was a little worried.

"They should be here by now . . . she ought to have found one of them on the next block."

"Oh, that's the kind of force you have, is it?" said Odysseus. "Ah, there they come!"

He pointed down the street, and the man stretched his neck to see. Odysseus helped himself to his knife.

"Where'd you say? I can't make out a sign of them."

Odysseus rose nimbly to his feet.

"On second thought, my friend, neither can I. If you'll move off a few paces, I'll pick up my bundle. When the young woman arrives, please convey to her my admiring regard."

The man started up, pugnacious, but Odysseus had him by the throat, with the point of the knife under his chin.

"One word out of you, and in it goes! Swear to keep still, or I'll skin you alive the next time I come! . . . Nod your head!"

The choking man nodded his head, and Odysseus permitted him the use of his windpipe.

"Now you may go indoors and stay there for half an hour. After that, make all the noise you like."

He turned to pick up his bundle, but the man had no intention of letting him get away.

"Help! Sp——"

The vowel in the last word died into a groan as Odysseus got his thumb on the windpipe again.

"What's all this?" said a singularly appealing voice. Odysseus turned and looked at the most beautiful woman in the world. He recognized her at once. Desperately he hoped his disguise was perfect. With her came the girl.

"This fellow is a Greek spy, madam. I sent Adraste for the police."

"So she said. I thought I'd look at him. Now we'll all go in, before the neighbors join us."

She went through the door first, and the girl next. Odysseus insisted that the man precede him. In fact, he had some idea of not following at all. Helen noticed the pantomime.

"Both of you come, and stop that nonsense!"

Odysseus entered, and the slave ostentatiously bolted the door.

"Now," said Helen, "why do you think he's a Greek spy?"

The slave testified eagerly.

"He came here armed—he has a sharp knife on him—and he knows the Greeks personally. You should hear what he said about Agememnon and Men——"

He stopped embarrassed. Helen was amused. She turned to Odysseus.

"So you have the pleasure of knowing my first husband?"

"No, madam. I am a humble rug merchant from the East. But before the war I had the honor to display some of my wares for sale in your husband's house, in Sparta."

"Did he buy any?"

Odysseus saw a trap.

"Madam, I regret to say he did not."

Helen thought a moment.

"Was I there at the time, or was it after I had left?"

Again he suspected a snare.

"Madam, the date of your leaving is not known to me."

Helen shook her head.

[30]

"It must have been afterward. If I had been there, he would have bought one. I've always had a weakness for rugs. You came at a bad moment, when he was breaking up housekeeping."

The slave interrupted.

"Madam, this fellow is a spy. Why don't you hand him over to the city at once? Your life may not be safe with him."

Helen laughed.

"Are you a spy?" she said. "You do look awful enough to be anything."

"Madam, I'm a rug merchant. In the matter of looks, I confess I don't qualify as a member of this household." He made a rather courtly bow toward the slave.

Helen gazed at him with sudden keenness. That last remark of his was a mistake.

"In your travels, did you ever meet Odysseus?"

With the girl and the slave listening, he couldn't say no.

"Once or twice, madam, very casually."

"That man is a puzzle," she said. "What quarrel had he with Troy? He cared nothing for me."

[31]

She paused, but he declined to comment.

"I'm afraid he's a cheap adventurer—wouldn't you say?"

"Madam, you may know him—I don't."

"Why, you stood up for him, a while ago," cried the slave. "You said he had abilities!"

Odysseus appeared to be racking his memory.

"I don't place the reference. He may have abilities. I don't know him well enough to be sure."

Helen put an end to the debate.

"I wish a word with this man in private. You two may wait here in the hall. . . . Come."

Odysseus followed her into an inner room—her boudoir, he assumed, but in so fine a house he wasn't sure. She made herself comfortable on a divan. He stood respectfully before her. Slowly she began to smile.

"Why are you here, Odysseus?"

"I am a simple merchant from the East," he began.

"Don't be frightened," she said. "I know who you are."

He took a convenient seat near by. His legs were weak.

"Well," he said, "I'll tell the truth, to save time. I'm trying to find out how to unlock the city gates."

"They don't unlock from the outside."

"Exactly. I want to know how to unlock them from the inside."

She was puzzled. He hastened to explain.

"The war's about over. A few of us are coming in, some night before long, and we'll open the gates for the others. I'm making the arrangements now."

"How will the first of you get in?"

"That's the secret."

"When's it to be?"

"That's a secret, too. You shouldn't expect me to tell."

"I just wanted to be ready," said Helen. "It can't happen too soon."

He looked surprised. "Your husband won't treat you well, when he gets his hands on you."

She smiled, unembarrassed, so far as he could see, and unafraid.

"He will kill me. That, too, can't happen too soon."

"You seem rather low in your spirits," said Odysseus. "We thought you were enjoying Troy."

"You know how it is," said Helen, "after you become used to a place. Until Paris died it wasn't so bad, but now they think of nothing but the war. It gets on your nerves."

Her manner was confidential. Odysseus forgot that he was a spy, in peril.

"I never thought much of the Trojans myself," he said. "Humdrum characters, most of them. Paris was an exception."

"I don't know—when you came to know him, he wasn't so different."

Odysseus watched her for a moment. She really was more beautiful than ever. It wasn't simply her face or her queenly body, those eyes and those lips, that graceful neck Menelaos had once called swanlike, that astounding bosom, those long white arms and legs—there was something besides, an energy within her, a sense of upwelling life. . . . He didn't care how long he talked with her.

"Odysseus," she said, "is my husband determined to kill me?"

"I'm afraid he is."

She didn't show much concern—she had asked as though to verify the weather.

"Then he ought to come soon. The fighting does no good. I'm sorry to see so many people die."

"Oh, it isn't your fault, not entirely," said Odysseus. "There would have been a war anyway. You just happened to be the cause."

For the first time she seemed annoyed.

"On the contrary, if I weren't here, they wouldn't fight another minute. That's why I ought to give myself up."

"You're wrong," he said. "No one ever appreciates a sacrifice of that sort. A war has to be fought to a finish, no matter how casual the origin of it."

She looked at him hard.

"You're an interesting man. Do you know, you're the only one who never, at any time, thought well of me."

"But I did. I do." His eyes took in her whole appearance. "I do at this very minute."

[35]

"No, you were always complimentary, but I guessed what you really thought."

"I wonder if you did!" He was rather proud of this remark, it sounded so well without committing him to anything.

She smiled. He asked himself what she was leading up to.

"Odysseus, I know exactly what you thought. You classed me among all the other women you know, as a pleasant amusement when you are in the mood for that sort of thing. Nothing to lose your heart to or to die for."

She looked her most radiant, and he fished around in his mind for an appropriate tribute. She recognized the effort.

"No, you probably had a delicious quickening of the pulse when you talked with Adraste, a few minutes ago—and if I cared to flirt with you now, you'd like that too. That's what you think of me. But I can't understand why, feeling no more deeply, you came to Troy."

"It's a long story," he said. "I shan't bother you with it now. Some other time, perhaps——"

"There'll be no other time. Menelaos will kill me."

"That's true. I'd forgotten your husband. Well, you can be sure of one thing, I didn't come out of any hostility to you."

"Of course not. You don't care one way or the other."

He couldn't help looking at her, and the impression was unavoidable that she was trying to make some sort of effect on him; her manner of disposing herself on the divan was really too luscious. Perhaps she hoped to seduce him. From all that he'd ever heard of her, he would have thought it probable, except that it didn't seem exactly the time or the place. He regretted that they had met when he was busy being a spy.

"You *don't* care—do you?"

He tried to return her gaze without feeling susceptible.

"Well,—you know how beautiful you are, Helen,—and I won't pretend I'm not a man."

Her eyes now were deeply thoughtful. This wasn't flirtation—the woman was in earnest.

"Odysseus, do you care enough to do me a great favor? I've no right to ask it of you, but you could do it better than any one else."

"What is it?" He wanted to be sure first.

"Take a message to my husband. You can tell it in the proper words. The other spies who have come in here were all a bit vulgar—I couldn't trust them with my personal affairs. Tell Menelaos the war can stop. I'm ready to surrender. He can do what he likes with me. If he'll send a herald over to-morrow, offering to take the army back to Greece on condition that the Trojans give me up, I'll tell the people here not to fight any more. I'll go back with the herald, and you can start for home to-morrow night."

He felt his spirits sink. She really wasn't going to flirt with him. Besides—what about the wooden horse? Was she going to monopolize all the credit for this war—for stopping as well as for starting it?

"I'd like to do any favor in reason, but this isn't so simple as you make it. The Trojans have an account to settle, aside from you. If you want to, you can surrender yourself—it's one way of committing suicide. But we're going to punish the city."

She wasn't impressed. He wished she wouldn't look as though she knew so much.

"Odysseus, the Trojans have spies, too. They have good reason to believe that if Troy offered to give me up, on just these terms, my husband and my brother-in-law would jump at the chance. In fact, the city council has voted to make the offer. I'd rather surrender myself than be turned out that way. If you'll take my message, I can go to my death with a little dignity—that's the only difference. Otherwise it comes to the same thing."

"When do they expect to make the offer?"

"It depends. They voted to do it at once. I got Priam to agree to wait till next Monday. Sunday's the anniversary."

"Of what?"

"I knew you wouldn't remember. Of our wedding, of course—Paris's and mine."

"What's that got to do with it?"

[39]

"I made Priam understand that I'd like to visit Paris's grave, for the last time."

She sounded so cheerful about it that he had to grin, and she smiled back, completely frank. He made a calculation.

"Couldn't you visit the cemetery two or three times, and delay the offer till Wednesday?"

She shook her head.

"I tried, but Monday's the latest."

"Then I can't do anything for you. That is, I can't take your message. But I suspect we shan't accept the offer now—it's too late."

"You mean, my husband won't."

"On this subject, Helen, I'll have to vote with him."

"Oh, no, you won't!" She walked gracefully but quickly toward the door. "On Sunday, for the sake of old times, I'll bring flowers for you too."

She turned to give him a last chance. He steadied his nerve and got his wits together.

"If we could talk this out a bit further, Helen——"

"No. You do what I ask, or the police will have you."

"Helen, give me five minutes to explain. I know what I'm about. If you listen to me, you won't have to surrender, and the Trojans won't give you up!"

She came back toward him and stood waiting.

"It all depends on the wooden horse."

"The which?"

"In a day or so you'll see a monumental horse outside the walls. When it appears, the Greeks will be gone. The Trojans will no doubt bring the thing into the city. It will be suitable for any of the larger temples. . . . Well, that's about all. The war will be over, and you can go where you please. Isn't that better than being executed by your husband?"

She narrowed her eyes at him.

"If I recall your first remarks, a few of you are coming in, some night before long, to open the gates for the others. You're making the arrangements now. All you need is to find out how the gates are unlocked from the inside!"

[41]

He flung himself on his knees before her.

"Helen! Kill me if you want to—afterward— but give me a chance with the wooden horse! It's the climax to my career! You've no idea the thought I've put on it! If you spoil it now—well, I might just as well never have come to Troy!"

She laughed, but she didn't open the door. He took courage from her delay.

"You're like all the other men. The largest part of you is vanity. What are a few lives, more or less, compared with the success of your silly stratagem? You can end the war with a word, but you prefer to risk your neck to prove yourself an inventor! I'm sorry. I can't countenance any more slaughter. You'll have to do as I say."

"That's your last word, is it?"

"Don't you know it is? You're in my power, man. I can deliver you to the Trojans now, and get some credit for doing it, or I can take you to the gate, show you how to unlock it, let you go back to the fleet, wait till the horse is brought in, and then tell the public what's inside it. You see?"

"You might," he said, "and no doubt you're planning to betray us, one way or another, but you're not the only person endowed with wits. There's more than one way to——"

He didn't finish the sentence. The slave stuck his head in the door.

"Has anything happened, madam? I was worried about you, alone with that fellow. The city won't understand your talking so long with a spy."

"Look here," said Odysseus, "you're too insolent this time! Insult me all you like—I'm only a helpless stranger. But if you try it on this kind lady, you'll make me angry!"

"Madam," said the fellow, "with your permission, I'll now call the——"

"You'll do nothing of the kind," said Helen. "You've made a mistake. This is an ignorant but harmless barbarian, who sold rugs in better days."

"That's true enough," said Odysseus, "but your slave is right—we need the police. Call them, you!"

[43]

The man couldn't believe his ears.

"Call them! Your mistress and I have evolved a happy method of ending the war. She's going to elope with me."

The man looked at Helen, then at Odysseus, then tapped his forehead significantly.

"Of course," said Helen. "You should have recognized the symptoms earlier. Wait just outside the door, in case he becomes violent."

The man retired. Helen and Odysseus looked at each other. He was pleased with himself.

"As I was going to say, when he interrupted us, there's more than one way to use your wits. When the police arrive, they will find you talking to Odysseus, who has spent all his powers of persuasion to show you that you ought to surrender yourself and end the slaughter. You don't see it that way, but if the Trojan council will commit you to his care, he will escort you back to the ships, and will guarantee the departure of the Greeks. Not a bad day's work. Less picturesque than the horse, but perhaps even more memorable."

[44]

He thrust his thumbs into the armholes of his coat.

"Well?" she said.

"Well?" He imitated her tone. She made a gesture of resignation.

"I see it's no use," she said. "You *are* a little crazy, Odysseus. But perhaps I am, too, trying to control fate. You may do what you please. You may now leave my house and go where you like—or where destiny permits. As to what happens to me, I'll wait and see."

"You won't give away my secret?"

"There's no promise between us, none on either side. You take your chance, I'll take mine."

"If you'd go so far as to swear not to interfere with the horse———"

"If you'll take my message to my husband———"

He considered a moment.

"Is there a side door? I'll try the street."

She called the man.

"Take this beggar to the porch where you found him, and let him go."

•   •   •   •   •   •   •

[45]

In the early morning Odysseus told the council all about it, before breakfast.

"I think I can find the gate," he said.

"But do you know how to unlock it from the inside?" said Agamemnon.

"Certainly." Nothing was going to stand between him and his experiment. He'd find out about the locks, somehow.

"Well," said Agamemnon grudgingly, "I really didn't expect to see you again."

"Oh, it was easy enough. The city is demoralized. By the way, Menelaos, I met your wife. She's looking awfully well."

Menelaos withheld comment.

"If you talked with her, by any chance," said Agamemnon, "she probably knows all about the horse."

"Not a thing," said Odysseus. "She's up to her old tricks. While I was buying one of her rugs, if you'll believe it, she made love to me!"

Part Two

THE BREAD-EATERS

PART TWO

THE BREAD-EATERS

WHEN Odysseus told later of his adventures, he would touch lightly on the mischance among the Ciconians. About the Lotus-Eaters, too, he was not very specific. In each episode, as you might guess, women figured, the first he had met since the victory at Troy, a victory which to some degree turned his head. He was on his way home, but he was now a hero, and from many a minstrel singing before camp-fires or in hospitable halls, he had built up an attractive ideal of a victorious hero, homeward-bound. Some aspects of the ideal were, he would have been ready to admit, predatory; the best tradition of returning warriors in his day included sudden descents upon unprotected islands, ruthless slaughter of the males, immediate consoling of the females. In some

[49]

legends the hero would gather up the most satisfactory women as he went along; in others, he would abandon them, and they would grieve over his departure. Odysseus favored this version. Penelope was waiting for him, and an extra wife would be in the way.

His account of the Ciconians, therefore, needs interpreting. He says the wind blew him from Troy straight to Ismarus, where those unfortunate people lived. He destroyed their city—it really was only a village—killed the men, and divided the women and the other property among his followers. Then, he says, he told the crew to make off quickly with the plunder, but they wouldn't hurry—in fact, many of them were too drunk. They delayed till some relatives of the Ciconians came down from the hill country and took a severe revenge. In the fight a number of his best sailors were killed before they could get the boat off, and the plunder had to be left behind.

Well, what really happened was this. He spent several days looking for Ismarus, because the women there were said to be handsome.

"It won't make much difference," he told his men, "whether we get home a day late or early, and we might as well see this part of the world while we're here, since we probably shan't come back."

It was one of the most popular pieces of advice he ever gave. The sailors rowed cheerfully whenever the wind gave out, and their spirits were high when they pulled into the harbor of Ismarus and saw the whole population waiting at the dock to greet them. The women vindicated the rumor—they were tall and stately, with pronounced charms. The men were good-looking, too, but unfortunately for them, they had left their weapons at home. It wasn't what you'd call a fight; those that didn't save themselves by their heels were soon resting on the bottom of the harbor, and the visitors washed up and gave their attention to the social side.

Odysseus found himself in the arms of a nice girl, tall and vuluptuous, in her twenties or maybe thirties. He noticed that she was the type time hardly affects. Their introduction was informal, and they wasted few words.

[51]

"I shall always remember our meeting," said the hero, buckling his helmet under his chin. "I hope your husband had the good fortune to be among those who retired to the hills."

The girl was putting up her back hair. She laughed. "I doubt if he was."

Odysseus was shocked. "You're not pleased to think he's drowned, are you?"

She laughed again. "Who said I had a husband?"

"Ah!" said the hero. "In that case your behavior is all the more commendable. I was afraid you might object to our arrival here, uninvited— and you've been so much more hospitable than convention requires——"

"Don't mention it," said the girl. "We're accustomed to visitors, but they rarely are interesting. I knew a real person would come at last."

He thought a mild kiss would be the proper return for the compliment. She hugged him back so hard that he choked.

"Man, how I love you!" she whispered.

"My own emotions are unfathomable."

"I don't mind being captured by a hero—when I was a young girl I used to fear it might be by some ordinary fellow, a merchant perhaps, or a beggar in disguise. You know the sort of people who travel nowadays. But you may take me where you will—there's nobody I'd rather be a slave to."

"Oh," said Odysseus, "I don't want you to be a slave."

She flung her arms around him in another hug.

"You darling! Chivalrous! Mate of my soul."

A sailor stuck his head in the door.

"If you're nearly through, Odysseus, we'd better shove off. There's something going on in the hills—we hear drums beating."

"Good! Pipe all hands to the boat. I'll be there in half a second."

"Now!" cried the girl. "Don't let's wait!"

The sailor departed. The girl was following him through the door.

"See here," said Odysseus. "I hope we don't misunderstand each other?"

"How could we, dearest? Do hurry up!"

"But hang it, you're not going!"

[53]

"Not *going?*"

"Of course not. You don't think I'd abduct a helpless woman from her very hearthside, do you? I've my faults, but I know where to stop."

"But I want to go! You're mine! I love you!"

"Now don't let's be sentimental," said the hero.

"No, don't let's," said the girl. She had the door shut and locked before he could move. "It's a trick lock," she said. "Now nothing can separate us."

"My dear young woman," said Odysseus, "do you know what you're about? I must go with my men!"

He pushed her aside, quite roughly, and tried to open the door, but she had the secret of it. When the Ciconians from the hills burst upon the village and the second fight began, his men had to break their way in for a last-minute rescue. They knocked the girl senseless, and dragged the hero off just in time.

Well, that was the background, as it were, of the visit to the Lotus-Eaters. His men were too well disciplined to say much, but he knew he

[54]

hadn't added to his prestige. They were steering directly for Ithaca now, and no nonsense. But after nine days he recovered his spirits and remembered the Lotus land.

"If you men are interested," he said, "I don't mind stopping a day or so to let you see the country. An unusually fertile landscape, I'm told—that is, along the shore; farther in, the mountains rise abruptly to great heights. The origin is volcanic, of course."

The wind was down and the men were rowing. They let him talk.

"The main product of the country is a food which the natives gather from the trees. It can be brewed or distilled into a powerful drink, or, more simply, baked into a kind of cake or bread. Among the natives the consumption of meat is practically unknown."

One of the laboring sailors spat ostentatiously but accurately clear across the boat.

"The exports, that is, the drink and the bread, have increased in volume in recent years, since our people from the mainland have opened up this part of the world to commerce. I regret to add that the natives have not been improved by contact with our civilization. In fact, they are dying out. But one can still see, here and there, vestiges of their primitive state. A very simple, attractive race, I understand. They used to wear no clothes. Of course we've changed that, but in the remote districts, I'm told, you can still come on their ancient habit."

The men rowed stubbornly but attentively.

"If we *had* a moment to pass with them, for me their charm would lie in their innocence. They are a childhood race. Absolutely without those blemishes of character, those impulses to rivalry and competition, those unhappy acquaintances with fear and falsehood, which convert even our culture into a doubtful blessing."

His lecture made him quite melancholy. The sailors thought he was through talking. He took the tiller from the helmsman, and turned the prow toward shore.

"I can't bear to see you lose the opportunity," he remarked sadly.

Eurylochus, who had been steering, resigned his place without protest.

"If they're as innocent as all that," he said, "we'd better have a look at them. They won't last long. How'd *you* ever hear about them, Odysseus?"

But Odysseus had his eye on a distant beacon and his thought strictly on navigation.

The Lotus-Eaters had no dock, but they greeted the boatload cordially some hundreds of yards offshore. In a playful humor they swam out and climbed on board. Odysseus himself feared that innocence might go too far when the first of the welcoming committee came out of the water, five men and four women, soaking wet, of course, and not a stitch on. He was about to save the situation by a speech—pointing out, perhaps, the disadvantages of a simplicity so extreme—when the chief of the party wrung his hand in greeting, a large man with a wide smile, an impressively broad chest, and a grip like iron. The large man took the tiller away from him, and ran the boat very cleverly up on the sandy beach. In fact, they came in on the top of a great wave. To Odysseus and his men the trick suggested magic.

The hospitality on land was as he expected, except that he hadn't thought of being separated from his sailors. But the Lotus folk lived in airy pavilions or cabins, leafy roofs without walls, and each home was prepared, it seemed, to entertain one voyager. The hero was brought to a large house, perhaps a royal palace, and there treated immediately to a thorough bath, a complete anointing or greasing, and a native costume. They didn't always go naked—the crowd came up that way from the beach, but as soon as they could, they appeared modestly covered by three wreaths, one around the forehead, one around the shoulders, and one around the waist. They dressed Odysseus so. He felt bashful to face his men in such a plight, and would have rested longer on the palace mat, but the natives urged him out to the public square, where his followers were gathered. On every one of them, three wreaths. In Ithaca he had seen animals so garbed for sacrifice. He was glad the natives ate nothing but bread.

Absolutely nothing else. They had a splendid feast that night, in honor of the visitors. Odysseus and his crew sat in a wide circle, garlanded and supposedly happy, while the natives served them with dishes all made of that strange tree fruit, sometimes baked hard, sometimes pulpy, sometimes of the consistency of soup, but essentially bread—and washed down with a creamy-looking stuff which induced peaceful exaltation. Until they had drunk this last, his men looked at him critically, as though they might have a thing or two to say about the mess he had got them into, but once the brew was inside them, they accepted fate and showed a strong disposition to go to sleep. As Odysseus was led home to his hospitable mat, his last conscious thought was a speculation as to the effect of this diet on the figure. The boys and girls who had attended them at the banquet and at intervals had provided languorous dances, were delightfully slender, but all their elders were inclined to be fat. Some of the most rotund seemed proud of their swelling persons. Penelope, he recalled, had severe things to say of middle-aged husbands who permitted themselves to get out of training.

Next morning he breakfasted on more bread, but drank only water. He wished to see the country, for exercise as well as for curiosity. When he intimated his desire, his host showed gratification, and at once assigned as his personal guide a young girl of the house, a flower-like creature, sinewy and straight as a tree. He called her Daphne, and she didn't seem to mind. Daphne was twenty, or thereabouts. This being a working day, she had left off the wreath around her shoulders and the fillet from her brows. Odysseus decided they would take a long walk.

Chiefly along the shore, of course—no point in climbing the steep cliffs. They wandered through enchanting forests or jungles, singularly green and secluded, and now and then they'd emerge on a clean sandy beach. Daphne ran ahead to show the way. Odysseus reflected that he had never beheld beauty so agile nor so brown. He followed easily.

In one of the glimpses of beach they rested.

"How do you spend your time," said Odysseus, "when you're not entertaining visitors?"

"There's enough to do," said Daphne. "Swimming—and dancing—and we have to gather the food.—Do you know how to walk up a tree, holding on by your hands? Strangers never do. I'll teach you.—And every day, of course, we have to make new clothes. Don't flowers fade quickly!"

Dear innocence! Odysseus was moved by the vision of a heart so white. He reflected sadly on the condition of his own spirit, burdened with culture and duty and general information, world-weary.

"But even at that, you must have considerable leisure."

"Oh," said Daphne, "when I've nothing else to do, I dream."

Odysseus smiled. "And what about?"

"Happy things. Of course, chiefly about you."

A bit strong, even for innocence! He looked sharply at her. She leaned over and touched him, with a tender, confiding gesture.

"You know, I've always dreamed of loving a king."

He drew a long breath and put on what modesty he could.

"My child, how did you guess I was a king?"

She might have answered that he looked like one, or that he had a royal point of view, or that there was a subtle air about him. He was prepared for anything. But instead she turned terror-stricken.

"Don't tell me you're one already!"

"Well, in a sense—when I'm at home. I'm the king of Ithaca."

"Oh!" She was obviously relieved. "If it's only in Ithaca, it probably won't count here. We'll keep it a secret."

"My child," said Odysseus, "a king in one place is a king everywhere."

Daphne shook her head. She was amused. "We don't do it that way. You aren't a king here. Not yet."

"I'm glad you hold out hope," said Odysseus. "I dare say I can wait. The idea is novel, but a seasoned traveler always follows the custom of the country. .. . . So you dream of loving a king."

Daphne looked up, happy again.

"They promised to let me marry the next one, and it's almost time now. I've waited ever so long, and so many other things would have been pleasant to do, but now I'm glad I was patient. I didn't dare hope the king would be like you. They usually are only—well, you know."

"I really don't," said Odysseus. "What is the average king like?"

"Oh, like some of your men. Whoever happens along. Nothing you'd choose with your eyes open."

Odysseus thought of Agamemnon and other colleagues.

"My men are above the average—I chose them with my eyes quite open."

"But you know what I mean," said Daphne.

"I think I get the point. . . . And you've dreamed of marrying a king like me? Hm . . .. Would you mind telling me why?"

[63]

Daphne looked as though the matter were too obvious.

"I want a child, of course. If I didn't have a child, I'd be awfully disappointed."

"My dear young woman! . . . But, you know, a king isn't strictly necessary—if a person of your charms wants a child, there's usually no reason why she shouldn't have one."

"I've set my heart on a king," said Daphne. "It's good luck."

He was glad she had fallen into the hands of one who could appreciate the perfection of innocence. Suppose she had taken a walk with one of his men! He resolved to protect her as long as he stayed. After that she'd have to take her chance. But he did wish there were more like her in the world, ignorant, if you choose, but unsullied. In comparison, what could be said for experienced women, the kind he had hitherto known? Helen was beautiful, but on the other hand—— And that Ciconian girl. Brazen thing! He blushed to think of her, in Daphne's presence. Even Penelope herself—a good woman, and all

that, but overprudent, not to say suspicious.
Jealous, too. He wondered how Daphne acted
when she was jealous. These primitive women,
he had heard, were inclined to be tigerish. Well,
she wouldn't know about Penelope. . . . Unless some of his men should blurt it out.

"Daphne, perhaps I ought to tell you, in fair-
ness, I've a wife in Ithaca, waiting for me."

Daphne looked deeply sympathetic.

"She's very beautiful?"

"Hm . . . well enough."

"Poor woman, I'm sorry for her—so lonely—
and she'll have to wait so long!"

"She'll wait," said Odysseus. "I just wanted
you to know all about my past."

"But you've met other women too, haven't you?"

"None to speak of," said Odysseus. "I've been
busy, and essentially I'm a man's man. It may
have been my fate." It was time, he thought,
for a personal tribute. "I may have been waiting
for you, without knowing it."

For a moment she seemed slightly depressed,
but her cheerful manner returned.

"Did your wife have a child?"

He ascribed the indelicacy to her ignorance, and forgave her.

"One son," he said. "A young man, by now."

Her warm arms were about his neck. "I'm so glad you've come at last!"

For a brief second his impulses were those of too civilized man, who knows more than is good for him, but she repulsed his kisses—postponed them, rather. Another occasion, apparently, would suit her better. The best part of his nature was humble, contemplating her instinctive wisdom. Yes, she saw more clearly than he the possibilities of a great love, a passion built up slowly on intimate companionship, communion of spirit, exchange of interests, sharing of thoughts, habits, memories. No other woman had so made him realize the latent powers of his soul. And without discounting the senses, with which the soul is unfortunately burdened. As his eye traversed all that brown slenderness, he perceived that it was the plan of heaven for him to tarry a while and be king and justify this maiden's high expectation.

He foresaw it would be a training in the more sublime values. And who can resist his destiny?

When they gathered for supper in the village that evening, the thought occurred to Odysseus that each of his men must have been taking a walk too. No longer did they monopolize the circle, with the natives gathered behind, but by every sailor sat a charming girl—charming in appearance, that is, but in behavior unfortunately bold. No one else seemed shocked, but to Odysseus, fresh from the uplift which Daphne's innocence had imparted, it was not agreeable to watch so much public flirtation. His men at their food were positively embarrassed by so many clinging arms around their necks, and frequently they had to stop drinking to accept a kiss. Odysseus reflected that amorous deportment is never pleasant to look at; if you are not engaged in it, you should be elsewhere. He would take the question up with his men at their next conference.

But pleasant or not, if it happens under your eyes, you can't ignore it altogether. Daphne by his side wasn't missing a thing. He remembered

[67]

what he had said just before landing, that civilization had brought to the savages nothing but harm. Who could tell how much bloom her innocence was losing as Eurylochus and the others set her this vulgar example?

Turning his troubled eyes from her to the girls less well behaved, he noticed with some surprise that they varied in color. Daphne was brown, an exquisite shade, but still brown. The shameless girls who seemed to share her ambition but weren't waiting for a king, were comparatively white. Until that moment he would have said that the whole tribe had the same skin. He made a note of it. He even had it on his tongue to ask the chief, when the meal came to an end. The effect of the drink was such that he just contrived to find his mat before his eyes closed. Daphne saw him safely home and said good night on the door-step. The other girls did likewise—at least he observed them starting off, each with her sailor.

The next day Daphne appeared to take him for another walk. He would have preferred a rest, for various reasons, but clearly she wanted him to come, and he hated to tell the energetic young thing that at his age such strenuous exertion over rough country produced an ache in the legs. The plains of Troy had been comfortably flat.

"Don't let's walk so far to-day, Daphne. We needn't explore the whole country at once. Let's save up some novelties for later."

"I'll show you the place where I always swim," said Daphne. "You swim, don't you?"

"Rather than drown, I do," said Odysseus, "but I hadn't thought of it as a pastime. Your people have a strong resemblance to fish. The day we arrived they came thrashing out to meet us like porpoises."

"I was there," said Daphne. "We picked you out then."

"I beg pardon?"

"For our next king. Everybody said you'd do extremely well, as soon as you were fatter."

This remark affected Odysseus unpleasantly. The girl wasn't so charming as she had seemed the day before. He examined her with care. . . . Yes, as a matter of fact, she was. Of course she hadn't meant to be rude. If her people went in for weight, she wouldn't know any better.

"In my country," said Odysseus, "my figure corresponds to the ideal measurements. It's simply a question of what you're accustomed to, I suppose. We like to see the muscles distinctly, in the arms and in those other areas where age tends to obscure them. A king ought to look approximately like this."

She stopped and turned back to contemplate him, standing in a sunlit glade. He made his biceps as conspicuous as he could, inflated his chest, lifted his diaphragm. Then he raised his arms and gave her a view of his knotted shoulders. She resumed her path through the jungle.

"When you do that," she said, "your ribs show. Our kings don't look hungry."

The subject wasn't worth pursuing. He was sorry she had brought it up, only because he knew he must choose sooner or later between starvation and obesity. That second supper had convinced him. Too much starch. If he could contrive a little variety, a bit of broiled meat, a sip of wine, pure sour wine——

They had come to her swimming beach, a strip of sand and a deep shelving bottom. He resolved not to go in. For the moment, at least, she was willing to stretch herself on the sand, in the hot sun. He wondered what she was thinking of. She rolled over and looked at him.

"Didn't they have a lively time last night?"

"Who?"

"Your men and the girls."

"Daphne, I was thoroughly ashamed of them. My men knew better—they should have set a good example. Knowing your fine ideals, I was doubly mortified."

She opened her brown eyes at him.

"What were you mortified about?"

"They drank too much, and they weren't polite. Hugging and kissing that way, in public."

Daphne considered. "I see what you mean. Perhaps they should have gone home sooner. But of course we don't find anything wrong in it. You must come from an awfully queer country. You must hate to love each other."

Odysseus felt his heart drop out of him. His innocent girl!

[71]

"Daphne! Don't tell me you——"

He couldn't go on. She lay on the sand, looking up at him, quite puzzled.

"Don't tell you what?"

"Daphne—you—you wouldn't behave like that with other visitors, would you—if I hadn't come? You never did, did you?"

Daphne sat up and laughed.

"Of course not! I told you I was waiting for a king. If you do that, the king won't marry you. . . . You know, I used to wonder whether it was worth waiting for, but now I'm glad I did."

"I'm relieved to hear," said Odysseus, "that the king is expected to be fastidious. There's something to be said against the extreme generosity of primitive manners. With time I hope I can explain to you the indirect advantages of social standards. The behavior of the sailors and those women is tolerable only so long as you know it's vicious. To consider it innocent is to render it disgusting."

Her expression told him she didn't know what he was talking about. In some degree she was bored. She rose to her feet, dropped the garland from her waist and walked toward the water.

"You're coming in, aren't you?"

"Not just yet. I'll wait and watch you."

She hesitated. "I don't want to leave you," she said. "You promise to stay here and watch?"

He promised, but he wondered how she thought he could do anything else. She went in as straight as a blade, with no more splash than a pebble would make. He was thankful she hadn't seen the tidal wave he always caused. For some reason she didn't swim far out—she moved up and down the coast with an easy gliding motion, one arm out in front, then the other, and under the water he could see her body bending. Perhaps the bending had something to do with the speed.

She sprang out of the water almost as easily as she had gone in, shook herself as a dog will, and lifted her arms above her head in a lazy stretch. He couldn't take his eyes off her.

"Daphne, I noticed last night that some of those other girls aren't so brown as you are."

[73]

"Not nearly," said Daphne.

"How do you account for it?"

"Sailors," said Daphne. She was adjusting her garland. "Or their grandmother may have married a king. I shall be the first woman in my family." She looked at him, suddenly happy. "Our child will be that queer color, too."

"Ah, I see," said Odysseus. "Very stupid of me. . . . But don't you ever have a king from your own people?"

"Of course not! He'd be of no use at all."

Odysseus agreed, but he hadn't expected her to see it. He passed several moments in deep thought.

"You mentioned the sailors. The king part of it I can understand, but I wonder if I got your idea about the rest. Did you mean that the mothers or grandmothers of these young women— er—I hesitate to put it into words——"

Daphne looked surprised at his obtuseness.

"They got their children from sailors—as the girls are doing now."

"I wish you wouldn't put things so plainly,"

[74]

said Odysseus. "You give me an abrupt sinking feeling."

"Why, what's the matter with that?" Her amazement was so genuine, he had to smile.

"My dear child, you've a great deal to learn, but ignorance isn't your fault—in fact, it's one of your charms. But in my country the best families wouldn't be gratified to watch their daughters falling into the arms of every boatload of strangers."

"We aren't either," said Daphne, with a touch of indignation in her tone. "You talk as though we weren't particular. It wouldn't happen at any other season of the year, but now it's just the right moment for the trees. Two weeks sooner or later, and no one would have looked at your men."

"I'm completely in the dark," said Odysseus. "If anything I said annoys you, forgive my clumsiness, but you needn't take your revenge by talking nonsense. It's the right moment for the trees, is it? What's the best season for mountains?"

"We'll go home now," said Daphne. "I don't like the way you talk to me."

No mistake about her being offended. She

started through the jungle with dignity and considerable speed. Odysseus followed in silence. He was willing to apologize, but first he hoped to find out what it was all about.

As they moved along, a small creature shot across the glade—a rabbit, Odysseus guessed. Having no other weapon, he seized a stone ready at his feet, and threw with sure aim. Two inches more to the right and he would have hit the thing on the head. Daphne had stopped; she glared at him with flaming anger.

"So that's the sort of man you are! You almost killed it!"

"Almost," said Odysseus. "I did my best."

"You come from a strange people," said the girl. "You like to kill a helpless animal! What good would it do you?"

"It would improve my diet," said Odysseus, "and indirectly my temper. One can't flourish for ever on bread, at least I can't. That helpless animal would have justified its existence in a stew."

The girl was horrified.

"It's murder! And blood on you! Say you don't mean it!"

"Certainly I mean it. At Ithaca this very moment they're probably sitting down to a fine roast. I wish I were there."

"So do I! We shan't let you be king! I don't want to marry you!"

She turned and fled from him, and he after her. Perhaps it wouldn't do to let her burst into the village in this state of mind—the chief might suspect she hadn't been treated well.

"I say, Daphne, I'm sorry I offended you. . . . Stop a moment, won't you?"

She fled on.

"All right. Good-by! I'm not going back."

She turned at once, and hurried toward him as fast as she had fled.

"Of course you're going back! What would they do to me if I came home without you?"

"If you tell them all my shortcomings, they'll probably congratulate you," said Odysseus.

"But they have to have a king."

"I thought I didn't qualify. I don't know a

thing about the right season for trees, and I crave meat."

She looked at him seriously a moment. "In a king, after all, it doesn't matter so much. I shan't say a word about it."

Her smile came back. It was as though she had never been angry.

"Now that's the right spirit, Daphne. And I withdraw anything you don't approve of. I'll even try to survive on bread. But I do want to learn about trees. In my country we have none to mention—chiefly rocks."

"I supposed every one knew," she said. "That's why I thought you were poking fun at me. But if you don't know how to make a tree grow, no wonder you have nothing but rocks. You see, when a tree is planted—we've just finished our planting—it won't grow well unless there's a great deal of life starting all around it."

"That's a rather poetical idea," said Odysseus. "Trees do well in an atmosphere of love, is that it?"

"Precisely."

"Upon my soul!" He was moved to laughter, but prudence kept his face straight. Daphne was still sensitive. "Let's go on home," he said. "I've learned enough for one day."

They walked on, friendly enough, but he felt he ought to lay a parting word on the subject, a gesture to bury it once for all. "Yes," he said, "that's as fine an example as I know of primitive poetry."

"It's common sense," said Daphne. "You people who fight wars and kill animals and can't swim and don't know the first thing about the secret of life, you drop in here and call us primitive. Don't you feel a little foolish?"

"I do, as a matter of fact."

She took the admission kindly—in fact, she waited till he caught up with her, and from there on she clung to his arm affectionately. When they strolled into the village they were leaning on each other's shoulder in an advanced state of sentiment.

But during the evening meal, as Odysseus cast his eye around the happy circle, he was heard to

sound a low chuckle once or twice, what was left
of a suppressed guffaw. The fit came on him
again afterward, when he observed Eurylochus
going to his rest, escorted by a tan-colored girl.

"Eurylochus," he called out, "how's the orchard
doing?"

Eurylochus and the girl hurried over to him,
solicitous and sympathetic, and insisted on seeing
him home.

He wouldn't have walked at all the next day, if
Daphne hadn't urged it. During the night he had
pondered the advisability of resuming the voyage.
If the men really became fond of these women, it
might be difficult to dislodge them. In previous
voyages he had found that the earlier the break,
the easier. But almost at dawn Daphne was pleading with him to visit a beautiful spot she had been
saving up, the most wonderful place in their
country. He confessed to excessive weariness, but
she wouldn't be denied.

"Yesterday," she whispered, "we weren't happy.
Now I love you again. Give me these hours, and
we'll forget. From this moment, nothing but love!"

Well, that sounded promising. They started quite briskly through the morning dew.

It was a long walk, this time, and the path ran up the mountain. Now and then he caught glimpses of the sea, and each time the water was farther down. His legs were getting weak.

"It's only a little more," said Daphne. She ran up-hill as nimbly as he could travel on the level; tired as he was, he enjoyed the sunlights on her smooth brownness as she flashed under the trees. "Here it is," she called.

It was a terrace, cut in the cliff-side—or perhaps one should say a palace; there were rooms, galleries, windows—he couldn't take it in all at once. Far below rolled the brilliant sea.

"It's yours!" she cried. "I asked them if I might show it to you first. They let us come to-day."

"Mine? What's mine?"

"The palace. This is where you'll live when you're king. You and I."

He took another look at it, then at the waters below, then at the palace again, then at Daphne.

[81]

The climb hadn't wearied her—if her heart fluttered a little beneath that lovely breast, it wasn't from the swift ascent, he knew—she flung her arms around him and pressed her body to his.

"You and I! And then our child!"

He carried her over to a soft green spot in the terrace. It never occurred to him that a hero and a king could do less, and he thought he recognized her mood. But she pushed him away, and in her eyes he saw reproof.

"I thought you loved me," he said.

"I do—I do—but I mustn't until you're king. Didn't I tell you?"

"Well, how soon am I going to be king? Can't your people hurry it up?"

He had never seen her so delighted.

"Oh, do you *want* them to hurry? How noble of you!"

"Not at all," said Odysseus. "The sooner the better. Let's go down again and have it done to-day. Then we'll come right back."

Daphne considered a moment.

"It takes a little time—but maybe they could.—

[82]

Oh, I wish they might! Come along and we'll see!"

She went down so fast he had some fear of her safety, and twice he twisted an ankle. The second twist delayed him a moment or two, and in that enforced pause he learned the last secret of the Lotus-Eaters. Daphne was rubbing his ankle, skilfully and affectionately, and he was gazing over her shoulder—for once not at it but over. His eye fell on a very large number of mounds or hillocks, laid out systematically along the foot of the cliff.

"What are those?"

She looked up, and he pointed. He thought she seemed embarrassed.

"You know what they are, don't you?"

"I do not."

"Why—they're the graves of our kings."

"So many of them?"

"Of course. One a year."

They looked at each other. She went on the defensive.

"No other country gives its kings so fine a

palace, or such wonderful graves. They're cut out of the rock. I knew you'd admire them."

His eye ran down the long row of mounds, too many to count. At the end of the series there was a hollow and a pile of newly cut stone.

"Is that a grave too?"

"Yes." She put her arms around his shoulders, laid her head on his bosom, and whispered very softly, "That one is yours."

It wasn't the first time in his life that Odysseus needed presence of mind. His fame rests on his gift for summoning it up at the right moment. Now you would have thought he had just heard some good word from home.

"I wish I knew more about your wonderful country," he said. "That's a finer grave than I ever hoped for. You've omitted nothing for my comfort. The program, as I understand it, is that I'm to be king at the earliest moment. Then you and I are to live in that remarkable castle—I needn't dwell on that part of my happiness. Shortly afterward I'm to die."

"Yes, as soon as I know there's a child."

[84]

"Of course. And if I understand the underlying philosophy, it's to bring on the trees."

"Well," said Daphne, "it's mostly for good weather, but that helps the trees too."

"Nothing could be clearer," said Odysseus. "Now, about this dying—do I arrange it myself, or is it tended to for me?"

"Oh, the priest will do that," said Daphne. "You don't have to bother about a thing. There's a wonderful procession to another place higher up on the cliff. We'll all go. It's over quickly, and the priest says it doesn't hurt. They stretch you out on your back, and the priest takes out your heart."

"If that doesn't bring on fair weather," said Odysseus, "I don't know what would. The way I feel, the sooner I'm king, the better I'll like it. Let's get on. My ankle is quite well."

She ran ahead. "You're a wonderful king!" she called back. "No one else was ever eager."

"Oh, that's the way I am," he said. He didn't speak again till they were on the plateau along the sea.

"Daphne, I'm embarrassed about one thing. The sort of king I'd like to be ought to know how to swim."

"It's not important."

"For my own peace of mind, it is. Let's stop a moment and see how well I do. Perhaps I'm all right,—if you say so, I'll feel better."

So they turned off and found the beach.

"I like the way you went in the other day," he said. "Just how did you do it?"

"Stand here," she said, "lean over a little, jump as high as you can, then turn down, straighten out, and keep your feet together. Like this!"

She was so lovely, he hated not to stay and watch her, but as soon as her toes had left the rock he was shoving through the jungle for his life.

He never knew why she didn't find him at once, she who traveled like the wind through that tangle. Perhaps she was sorry for him, and gave him his chance. Perhaps she cared nothing either way, when once he had shown himself a coward. Of course the village would miss him at supper-time. He pushed on along the coast, desperate and tired.

Toward evening he was hungry. Those bread trees didn't grow out this way. With every mile the ground grew flintier. He carried a sharp stone in each hand, against a sudden surprise. But nothing crossed his path except another rabbit. Of course he had promised to abjure meat, but for practical purposes all promises to Daphne were now void. This time he hit the creature square in the head. He felt better. Now if he could only skin it—and if he could strike a fire from those flints—he had heard of its being done.

He was in the midst of the skinning, not getting on any too well, and rather disgusted with the amount of blood on his hands, when an alien sound made him look up. There were the warriors of the village, every one of them, he guessed, pointing their spears at him in an uncordial circle. They didn't say a word, but they emitted a few grunts of disapproval at the blood on his hands. From the way they poked their spears at him, he judged he was invited to move toward the sea. It was no use arguing.

By the edge of the waters they waited a long

[87]

time—for what, he couldn't imagine. But at last a small boat, with two oars and a small water cask in it, appeared around the promontory. It was propelled by two youths from the shore; they shoved it awkwardly with long sticks, and when the boat was opposite the spot where he stood, they threw the sticks into the sea, as though their very touch were contamination. Odysseus saw what was expected of him. He waded out to the skiff, climbed in and took hold of the oars.

At that very moment, as he started to pull, a girl dashed to the shore and threw out a small bundle, a clumsily tied package. It fell into the boat, but he didn't stop to examine it till he was safely over the horizon. He found there—was it Daphne's love or her farewell irony?—a generous supply of soft dough.

PART THREE

CIRCE AND THE HIGHER LIFE

CIRCE AND THE HIGHER LIFE

ODYSSEUS understood that Circe was a dangerous woman. One more peril for him to get by, on the way home. It seemed a bit hard, after the Lotus-Eaters, and the Cyclops, and what-not. Would fate never let up on him?

So he stopped off on her island, to see how dangerous she was.

The landscape wasn't hospitable. A thick wood came down to the shore, a forest of pines and other dark green trees which made twilight all day, and suggested fear. One solid roof of boughs, one interminable carpet of scented needles, but no sign of a house, or castle, or whatever she lived in.

Odysseus kept prudently to the coast till he found a hill, a respectable rock. Perhaps from the top of it he might see where the estate lay—by

a lake, or in a clearing. . . . No, nothing but
trees. He wondered if it was the wrong island.
Even if it was the right one, Penelope, he remembered, had been waiting a long time. . . . Ah
yes, there it was, toward the north—a thin thread
of blue smoke, straight up out of the forest in the
quiet air. That's where the danger was. And
supper cooking. He fixed the direction in his
mind, and climbed down.

The walk through the wood was too silent to be
pleasant. He wished the ground were not covered
with needles—he would have felt more natural if
he could have heard his own footsteps. There were
no birds—always a bad sign. Once he did hear
a rustle—over to the left a tall stag with magnificent antlers was looking at him. He looked back.
Neither moved. He gave a sudden shout. The
animal, unstartled, stared a second or two more,
and walked away from him, very leisurely. He
mopped his forehead and went on. The noise he
had made unnerved him.

Half a mile farther he was suddenly aware of a
large dog, just where he must pass, unless he

changed his direction ignominiously. The beast was lying at full length with its nose in the pine carpet, and he noticed with regret that its eye was on him. He shook his sword loose, to be ready, and pushed on; motionless otherwise, the dog followed with that cold stare. Of course, when he had got well by, he had a sense that the thing might jump at him from behind. To make sure, he looked back. The dog was still watching. Odysseus walked a bit faster.

He had barely done another half-mile when he saw a man coming toward him, a tall young man, in great haste. As he drew near, Odysseus noted the soft mustache on his lip—yes, a very young man indeed, but unusually tall, and armed with an unnecessarily wicked sword. But the young man was less observing than the dog, didn't even glance at him, in fact was about to walk him down as though he hadn't been there.

"I beg your pardon," said Odysseus. "Really, you ought to beg mine, but we won't stickle over it."

The young man stopped, annoyed. "You're going the wrong way."

"Isn't this the way to Circe's house?"

"It is. That's what I meant." The young man was moving on.

"See here, friend, you don't mean anything sinister, do you? Is she dangerous?"

"As you may have noticed," said the young man, "I'm leaving the neighborhood. It's been postponed for a year. Would you mind stepping out of the way? Conversation was never so untimely. I'm late."

"Sorry to detain you," said the hero, "but I'd like your advice. I was thinking of calling on Circe. Of course I don't have to."

"The one before me didn't have to, either," said the young man. "Poor fellow!"

"Wait a minute! What does she do?"

"She tames you. A few days in this place, and you'll lose your ambition. I'm leaving."

"The animals don't seem tame," said Odysseus.

"Man, they're too lazy to stand up!"

"Do you know," said the hero, "the stag and the dog upset me. They suggested incantations, and transformings, and that sort of thing."

The young man looked at him sharply.

"Well, perhaps you've met some of the human ones."

"There now," said Odysseus, "I was afraid of it! She *does* throw a spell on you?"

"If you're really going to risk it, there's just one sure precaution. Here!" He went quickly to a mound in the pine carpet where a whitish growth, fungus-like, showed itself. "Here! Crush this in your hands, and when she offers you food, sprinkle it over the dish. That will do the trick."

Odysseus gathered a handful of the sovereign remedy, and tried to crush it. Evidently this specimen wasn't dry enough. He looked about for more—and then he realized that the young man had disappeared. Uncanny, that. . . . And the dog was gone too. . . . Perhaps they hadn't really been there. . . . Odysseus walked on, nervous, but rather glad the peril was so promising. In his hand he still clutched the white growth.

Her house wasn't so magnificent as he had expected; a sorceress, you'd think, would live either in a cave, or in a hut, or in a fairy palace. Circe

[95]

had just a house. A fair garden outside—nothing startling; a few vines up the southern wall and over the porch—he couldn't be sure whether it was honeysuckle or wisteria; modest curtains.

He wondered whether you knocked, or whether she foretold your arrival and came out to meet you. Some one was singing—not a bad voice. He walked cautiously to the nearest window and peeked in. There she was, seated at a table—he wasn't sure at first, but he thought she was—yes, she *was* doing a small piece of embroidery. Not what you'd expect of an enchantress. He wondered if he had stopped at the wrong house. If his eyes didn't deceive him, she was extremely young, tall, beautiful. It was the right house. At her feet lay two immense hounds, sleeping. More of her enchanted lovers, perhaps. Not very alert as watch-dogs, he must say. ⋅ ⋅ ⋅ He was so lost in the vision and the thoughts that he bumped his forehead against the window, and Circe looked up. He suspected that she wasn't pleased to see a strange man peering in. She must have given a signal, for the hounds woke suddenly and had their eyes on him too. . . . Embarrassing, but the best strategy, he recalled, is frankness. He stepped around to the front door.

Before he knocked, Circe had it open. She stood just behind the threshold, a hound on each side. He smiled with delight, and she frowned back at him—but he couldn't help the smile, at sight of such unusual beauty. Tall, indeed, and panther-like, he thought; if her favorite trick was to turn her lovers into animals, could it be that she was a creature of the wilderness, disguising for a while in a woman's body?

Tawny-colored, slow and lazy-seeming, guarding herself with her eyes—he saw a strong resemblance to the cat family, but didn't admit it to himself, since the charm of cats is an unheroic peril. A serpentine fascination would be better, but—he glanced at the single yet rich robe that depended casually from her shoulders and covered her bosom intimately—no, these fancies were wide of the mark. She was primarily a woman.

An angry woman, for the moment. "You must be proud of yourself!"

"Not particularly, madam. I was looking for Circe's house, and——"

"Well, you can't find it through the window. You're the first tramp that's gone through here in several months, and I'll say you're no credit to the profession. The honest ones try the front door first."

"I'm no tramp."

"Ah——then a pilgrim, perhaps? A disreputable fellow last year, no worse than you, gave that excuse."

"Madam, I'm only an unfortunate man, trying to get home."

Circe shook her head slowly. "I never heard that before. Why did they send you away?"

Odysseus was annoyed. It wouldn't do to assert himself, not to this woman, not yet, but if he didn't explain his situation, his visit would be—well, in the wrong key.

"I left of my own will, madam, to help out a friend. His wife had run away."

"They will, from time to time," said Circe. "What comfort did you prescribe?"

[98]

"I helped him to catch her again."

"When you peeked through the window," she said, "I knew you had a mean spirit."

Odysseus did the frowning this time, very spontaneously.

"Madam, my story is widely known. It is not my habit to boast."

"Don't," she said. "Save your wits till you get home. Who's been feeding the pigs while you were gone?"

"Pigs, madam?"

"I keep them myself," said Circe, "but the boy who takes care of them has just left. If you want to make yourself useful——"

"Madam," said Odysseus, "at home I am a king."

Circe laughed, a very haunting, soft, husky kind of laugh.

"None of the others," she said, "had so nimble a tongue, but essentially you're all alike. What you're after is food. I suppose I'll have to get you something. Sit down out here. The dogs will watch you."

[99]

What he was about to say would not have been polite, but before he could clear his throat she had disappeared, and it was no use wasting words on the hounds. He sat down. . . . Besides, if he lost his temper, she would have him at a disadvantage. His fate depended on the food. If he didn't accept it, she might set the animals on him, and if he did, he might find himself turned into a third guardian of the house, furry and four-footed. Or perhaps she'd send him out to be another sentinel in the forest, lying with his nose in the pine carpet. Not that he really believed those stories about her, but it was silly to take a risk. . . . He still had that white plant clutched in his hand, sticky and damp. Providential, you might say.

She came out with some cold things on a plate.

"Madam," he said, "I never should have found your dwelling if I hadn't observed smoke from your chimney. At least, I thought it was smoke."

She was dusting off her hands as though the touch of the plate had contaminated them.

"Your eyesight is excellent. It was smoke."

She was smiling a little. The two hounds stole up to the food, sniffed at it, and drew back, more than satisfied.

"I don't like to mention it," he began, "because you might think I didn't appreciate your hospitality, but——"

"They all prefer warm food," she said. "I knew you were going to complain. You'll eat up the cold things first, or you'll starve. Afterward—we'll see."

"See what, madam?"

"The pigs come next. If you show decent gratitude for this perfectly adequate meal, you can clean out the sty. If you do it thoroughly, I'll furnish soap and hot water, and you can wash up. If you then are presentable, I'll invite you to supper."

Odysseus studied the plate and considered.

"Take it or leave it!"

He unfolded from his fist the crushed plant, and tried to spread it out, to cover all the meat.

"What's that?"

"Madam, that is seasoning."

"It doesn't need any! You haven't tasted it yet."

He raised the seasoned food to his lips. Really, the plant was most unpleasant.

"That stuff is green," she said. "You must have found it near."

Odysseus saw an opportunity for discretion.

"It was, I might say, revealed to me, madam. I was already conscious of needing it, but probably should have passed it by if a sudden stranger, a godlike young man, had not appeared and put it in my hands."

"Godlike?"

"Madam, I'm not religious in the narrow sense, but any one with wide experience knows that providence may operate through what we would ordinarily call a human form."

"You think you met a god, and he gave you that nasty thing to eat?"

"Madam, I beg of you——"

"Was the god rather young?"

"Decidedly."

"A slight mustache?"

"Very slight."

[102]

"Well," she said, "the god was hard up, if he couldn't find a better form than that one. .₁ .₁ .₁ If you're through, I'll take the plate and you can get at the pigs."

Odysseus wiped his lips on the back of his hand and stood up.

"If I hadn't reason to be thankful for that casual meeting, I shouldn't venture to disagree with you, but I insist that the young man was providential."

"We won't quarrel over an adjective," said Circe. "I thought he was lazy. Perhaps it's the same thing. I had to discharge him just after lunch."

"He didn't mention that, but he said something or other was postponed for a year."

"I like his impudence!"

"The reference escaped me," said Odysseus. "I thought perhaps he meant——"

"I broke with him completely, and he thinks he'll get another chance. Lazy rascal!"

"Didn't he keep the sty clean?"

"He did not—but it wasn't entirely that." A meditative expression overspread her eyes, but she

[103]

roused herself. "Go round to the back of the house. There's a shovel, a hoe and a broom. In an hour I'll see whether you deserve the soap and water."

The number of the pigs was seven. Why so many, he couldn't guess. They were friendly creatures with caressing voices, four bass and three verging on baritone. They greeted him like an old acquaintance—in fact, got in his way. The condition of the sty was deplorable. He leaned on the hoe and wondered if the adventure was worth the trouble. . . .

"Unless you begin soon," said Circe, "you'll get no breakfast."

The seven pigs stood in a row and watched him begin. He thought they were smiling.

When he was ready for supper at last, he detected a more cordial manner in his hostess. The soap had made his forehead shine handsomely, and his beard, once the dust was washed out of it, resumed its distinguished curl. He was pleased to note that she had changed her working dress for a fabric finer and more subtle. The woman had a social gift—he could tell it from the way the table was set.

"This is very pleasant, madam, after the hardships of travel."

"Does it remind you of home?" said Circe. "That's the formula I hear most often."

"Ah, madam—home! Don't mention it."

"Why not?"

"It wrings my heart. My infant son—my lonely wife——"

"Will you have some more soup?" said Circe, "or shall I bring in the meat?"

Odysseus sat up very straight. "I was speaking of my wife and child."

"Then you won't have more soup?"

He wanted some, but preferred not to surrender.

"Well, if you don't mind I'll have some more," she said. "It's the best part of the meal."

He watched her while she ate it.

"My wife," he said, "is in a very difficult position."

Circe removed the soup plates and retired to the kitchen. The dogs kept their eyes on him till she returned. Perhaps—he flushed at the idea—perhaps they were trained to protect the silver.

"How do you like the meat cooked?" she asked, bringing it in.

"Well done, thank you."

"Why do men always like it that way? I like it red. Will you carve?"

He carved. It was red. In Ithaca he would have called it raw. Conscious of his duty as a guest, he tried to eat a small piece.

"She has been waiting for me for several years," he went on, "and unless some of my friends have notified her, she doesn't know whether I'm dead or alive. I call that hard."

"Do you care for salad?"

He meant to look at her sharply, but she was caressing one of the dogs, and didn't see.

"Do you?"

"As a matter of fact, I do, but it's not important."

"Exactly the way I feel about it. You can pick some in the morning, and we'll have it for lunch. Unless you're leaving after breakfast."

"I'm not sure yet how soon I shall leave."

She raised her eyebrows. "In any case, I suppose the table may as well be cleared."

He made no move to help her. "My various departures," he said, "have always depended on————"

She wasn't listening to him. She didn't ask him to continue his remarks. He coughed, to encourage himself.

"On a favorable wind."

"You *are* original, aren't you? Now, will you wash the dishes and I wipe them, or the other way around?"

"At home," said Odysseus, "my wife tends to all that."

"When you've got them washed," said Circe, "you'll find a towel over the sink."

Not another sound from her, till the last dish was put away. She was busy with her embroidery. He helped himself to a seat across the room.

"My son must be quite a man by this time. It's an extraordinary fate, when you think of it, to leave your son an infant and find him a grown man, perhaps impossible for you to recognize, unless a family resemblance persists. As a child, he was unusually handsome."

She turned the embroidery upside down, and studied the reverse.

"Time is a slippery thing. You wouldn't think me forty-five, now, would you?"

"I would not. At least sixty."

He sighed. "It's grief," he said.

She put the embroidery away and yawned. "You saw where I keep the garbage. The first thing in the morning, feed the pigs." Very gracefully she moved toward the hallway.

"Where shall I sleep?" said Odysseus.

"I don't care—please yourself."

"Before we retire, hadn't I better lock up?" He tried the front door.

"There's no key in it," she said. "There's not another soul on the island."

She disappeared into her room. One of the dogs took up a strategic position across the sill, the other stretched himself before the hero's armchair and blinked up at him. Odysseus wished there had been a sofa or a couch, but, after all, an armchair is something. He meditated on Circe and her hospitality, shifted his aching muscles and analyzed his emotions. Was she enchanting, or only seductive? Was he already under her famous spell, or was he sleepy?

Several months later he was still asking these questions. He began his days waiting upon the pigs; he ended them in pleasant but not spirited conversation with Circe, as she bent over her embroidery. His one sign of progress was the cot he now slept on, instead of the armchair, but it wasn't of her providing—he found it himself, ransacking the attic.

His evening talks with the panther-like lady were not, you might say, romantic; she answered when spoken to, if her attention wasn't too much on her work; she never uttered a syllable to imply satisfaction that he was there. Once he remarked:

"You've hear of the Lotus-Eaters, I presume."

"What if I have?"

"Oh, nothing. I stopped with them on the way here. My men all succumbed to their charms."

[109]

"What was the matter with you?" said Circe.

"I suppose it was the pull of home ties," said Odysseus. "If you eat the sweet fruit they have in that land, you stay for ever, you forget your duties, or if you ever leave, it's because some one puts you out."

"Who put you out?" said Circe.

"I didn't eat the stuff," said the hero. "I pleaded with my men till the tears came to my eyes. Then there was nothing to do but leave them. I hope my action will not be misinterpreted when I get back. I had no wish to abandon them, but really their case was hopeless."

"I guess they can bear up under your departure," said Circe.

Yet he hung on from day to day, convinced that there was the real thing in the way of adventure, if only he could get by her fascinating reticence. The rudeness of her manners he translated into a bewitching honesty of mind, and he suspected she was in love with him herself, but reluctant to admit it.

One night when he had washed and wiped the

dishes, and settled in his chair across the room from her, he had the impulse to bring his visit to some sort of conclusion. At the moment she seemed unusually handsome, and he regretted the distance between them, the tentative note in their companionship.

"As I've been going about my work," he said, "I've meditated recently on the social conventions between men and women."

"Assuming that there are any," said Circe, "what's the matter with them?"

She still worked on the embroidery, but this time she showed a spark of interest.

"They are false—too complicated, too cumbersome for the direct communication of soul with soul."

"You find it so?" She actually put down the embroidery and looked at him.

"A woman is brought up nowadays to think her chief business is to capture every man she meets, and the men think they've got to make love to all the women." He crossed his legs comfortably. "It's a great nuisance."

Circe resumed her work. "It must be," she said. "I'm glad I wasn't well brought up. I never try to capture anybody—not even the attractive ones."

He thought this over.

"My idea is that if men and women weren't accustomed to this bad tradition, they'd just be friends—that is, the sympathetic ones. Then you'd have a world of—well, it would be a much better world."

She paused again, and turned toward him. "They'd just be friends, would they? How would they go about it?"

"Why, they'd just be friends—nothing to go about."

She shook her head. "I never saw it happen, and I can't imagine how it's done. Have you ever been this simple kind of friend with anybody?"

"Frequently, frequently," said the hero. "In friendship you talk—exchange ideas—have the same enthusiasms—share your troubles—perhaps you pass the time in each other's company without a word, basking, if I may use the term, in mutual harmony of spirit."

"I'll begin at that end," she said. "I like silent basking." She thrust her needle through the cloth, and turned her back on him.

"When I referred to the higher life," said Odysseus, "I wasn't limiting myself to the mystic aspects. Harmony of spirit does not necessarily preclude conversation."

One of the dogs got up and stretched. Odysseus rose too, and walked up and down the room.

"If you took more exercise in the daytime," said Circe, "you wouldn't have the fidgets now."

He sat down again, and meditatively rubbed one leg. "My foot was asleep."

"Which foot?"

"The right."

"Then why are you rubbing the left leg?"

He began to rub the other. "At times," he said, "I think you really try *not* to be sympathetic. That's why friendship is so rare—women won't make the effort to understand—not the ordinary ones, anyway."

She turned so swiftly, he half expected her to spring at him across the room.

[113]

"*Don't* I understand? You think you're a mystery, do you? Well, every one that's been here was the same. First, a sheeplike admiration, then a rather nasty style of love-making—call it friendship or what you will, it comes to the same end—then a fine flare of passion, and then one more lazy, conceited animal loafing around the house. I never met a husband who got any further. You all want food, and then you want me, and then you put your feet up on a chair or a couch and think it over for the rest of your days!"

"An ignoble love," said Odysseus, "will transform the best of men into an animal."

"That's far from my experience," said Circe. "A really noble love might fit a man to associate with a fine dog. I've never seen it happen, but I suppose it would."

"My experience," said Odysseus, "is probably wider than yours. When I was at——"

"Why don't you go home to your wife?" said Circe. "The first night you were here you babbled about her, but recently I haven't heard her name. Doesn't she want you back?"

[114]

"My wife is a remarkable woman, and there are times when the yearning to see her again drives me to——"

"I can just imagine the sort you are when you're home. I get your wife's point of view without the least effort. Every day I keep you here, supplying you with food and mild distraction, I think how grateful she'll be."

"What sort did you say I was, when at home?"

"The good-for-nothing kind. You persuaded the poor woman you were going to be somebody. That was while you both were very young. She thought you would be a great lover. Then she thought you'd be at least a great man in public. Then she hoped you'd help with the housework. Then she got used to seeing you sit around, and she wouldn't even sigh when she had to ask you to lift up your feet so she could dust around your arm-chair. That's the way you've grown old."

Odysseus stood up. "I'm not old, and you've guessed all wrong. My gray hair is the result of sorrow and heavy thought, at Troy."

"Oh, that's where you did your heavy thinking,"

[115]

she said. "I knew it wasn't at home. Were there any women at Troy?"

"Several. The one I told you of, in particular."

"Poor thing! All that riffraff following her around!"

He stepped briskly to where she sat.

"You don't know the men you're talking about! You never in your life saw that kind. Yes, I'm old now, but when we first went there—as a matter of fact, I wasn't much in comparison with the others, but we didn't take insults, not even from women. Mind your tongue!"

She smiled bewitchingly at him, as if their repartee was of the happiest.

"Not insults, but you don't mind taking bread from women, do you? No, I didn't see your friends, but if you're a sample I can guess. You never did any real fighting—you just talked."

"My gift *is* for oratory," said Odysseus, "but I can fight on occasion. While Achilles was sulking——"

"One of those friends of yours, I suppose,—sulking."

He looked at her with sudden danger in his eyes.

"He's dead now—be careful what you say!"

She looked back at him, twice as dangerous. In fact, she strode over and spoke the words in his teeth.

"He was a cheap adventurer like you, a vagabond and coward!"

She was close to him, and it did seem as if she might unclinch her fists and scratch. That was his best excuse. Anyway, he slapped her face. Under his heavy hand she dropped to the floor. He thought of her dogs, a little late, and glanced about for a hasty weapon. But the animals were still in their place, blinking placid eyes. For them, apparently, this scene was not novel. Odysseus looked at the woman again, his knees wabbling. There was a bad spot on her cheek. She ought to put oil on it before it turned blue. He'd advise her as soon as she recovered consciousness. Her legs were bent under her, most uncomfortably, and her body, twisted in the fall, showed gorgeous through delicate cloth. Perhaps he had better lift her to the couch, let her rest easy. He leaned down and got his arms part way around her shoulders. There was a good deal of her—he staggered. But all beautiful. Delicious thing!

The delicious thing was roused by the pulling and hauling. She opened two dazed but lovely eyes and stared into vacancy. Gradually she recalled time and place, and at last recognized the beard and the blanched skin staring down at her. Her lips took on her most enchanting smile.

"Dear lover!"

"You'd better be careful how you talk," said Odysseus. "In general I don't like to hit a woman, but the memory of my friends is sacred. Achilles was a splendid gentleman."

"Of course he was! I don't know a thing about him, anyway. Dearest!"

"Your attitude has been faulty from the moment I entered this house. It isn't for me to boast of my career, but the first principle of hospitality is to treat the unknown stranger as though you suspected he might be somebody. A god in disguise, perhaps. Such things have occurred."

"It has occurred to me." She smiled broadly.

[118]

"You can't imagine what it is to be the victim of fate, to wander from coast to coast, at the mercy of the weather, to knock at doors, with you never know what behind them—friendship or hate or indifference; to wear rags and let them think you a beggar, rather than tell the truth about yourself and seem egotistical; to appear aged and dusty, the usual results of travel, though you have the heart and the eyesight of youth, and respond sensitively to everything worth while. This just isn't in your experience."

She took hold of one of his hands hanging limp, and squeezed it. He thought best to let the hand remain limp a second or two longer.

"And I must say, when a stranger comes to the house with a good mind and a taste for conversation on serious themes, it might be well to seize the opportunity. Beauty to the vulgar is a vulgar thing, wit to the shallow is merely funny, comradeship to the stupid is nothing but shelter in the same kennel, but the noble life, the higher life, to souls like——"

"Like you and me," said Circe. She stretched

[119]

up both her soft rounded arms, and her eyes were large and dreamy.

"I see what's on your mind," he said. "I've suspected it for some time, but our happiness will have a better chance of lasting if we agree that from now on you behave like a lady."

"God!" sighed Circe. "Sweetheart! Husband!"

"Husband if you like," said Odysseus. "No love is worth considering if it doesn't look eternal when it begins. But I've no faith in marriages founded on mere passion. Friendship, *I* say—and mutual respect."

For the time being, she proved an extraordinary wife. She stood by the fence while he tended to the pigs, and complimented him on his thoroughness. She insisted on drying the dishes after each meal, and they would sing together at their domestic tasks. That is, he found she expected him to sing, and he tried to meet her half-way. In the evening she encouraged him to talk, and frequently regretted that midnight came so soon, before he was half through his finest anecdotes. It wasn't simply the breadth of his experience, she would say—it was the original phrase he always found, and the constant play of mind; he translated the trivial into universal truth. And she wanted to hear of his friends—it helped her to imagine his background, it made her feel they had always been lovers. Helen and Bryseis she thought a little pale; his adventures on the way home excited her more. The Lotus-Eaters, for example, though she couldn't understand the purpose of the king-making—kings, like everything else in life, she contended, should be put to some good use. But the Cyclops delighted her. There, she said, was a person. Odysseus agreed, but added that the personality was excessive. Perhaps so, she admitted, but that was the encounter she would have best enjoyed.

The days, then, in true companionship, and the evenings passed in improving talk. Her affection did not decline. She persuaded him to let her wash the dishes—she disliked the growing roughness of his shapely hands; enough for him to wield the harmless towel. And she thought the pigs would prosper as well if cared for less systematically; perhaps an exaggerated culture might render them effete. So he cleaned the sty once a week.

At last, by gentle stages, she did the dishes entirely, while he rested after dinner, and the pigs cleaned themselves.

There are mysteries in love which man has not yet fathomed. Odysseus, wise for his time, could not understand why this steady increase in sympathy should not result in at least a maintenance of ecstasy. Circe was as beautiful as ever, in outward proportions, yet he detected a slight letdown somewhere. There was a subtle decline in the spell she cast. The food didn't taste so exquisite, her voice showed symptoms of monotony, her long hair was less carefully braided, her gowns—well, she hadn't many, and perhaps he had grown accustomed to them.

He found less need for talking in the evening. A few casual words, perhaps, always cordial, but when once he had got his feet up on the couch, his thoughts, he noticed, went off toward other moments, far away; particularly he remembered his youth, some insignificant passages of it which

[122]

curiously took precedence over heroic Troy and the distinction of the present moment. A bad sign, he feared. The back-looking mood betokens age.

Circe would speak to him, with a pleading kind of affection, and though the interruption made him irritable, she overlooked the impatience of his reply. Her approach had tenderness in it now, a motherly note. She was concerned about his health—a bad omen, if he had been shrewd.

"At least you ought to take a walk every day. Much as I hate to miss you for a moment, you ought to cover several miles before lunch. For my sake, dearest—to-morrow morning."

Odysseus yawned and stretched himself. "All right—you come along too—it'll do us both good."

"I can't to-morrow, but another day, perhaps."

"Good. There's no hurry. We'll go together some time."

"Dearest, for my sake—to-morrow."

You can't say no to a woman, when she's fond of you and means well. He started out in the middle of the forenoon, and for want of a better objective strolled over the path that had brought

him to Circe's house. He recognized the spot where
he had met the young man—and the watchful but
sedentary dog—and the self-possessed stag. The
pine needles still put silence under his feet, but
the spooky atmosphere of the forest had worn off.
Here and there a cheerful sunlight streamed down
between branches. . ., . And there was the rock
he had climbed, to catch a glimpse of the chimney
smoke. Well, he needn't climb it again. . . .
And here was the shore, and—yes, it was—the
boat as he had left it, months ago.

A pleasant thrill went through him, at sight of
that neglected hull. He examined the seams—
only one leak, and that not bad; an hour's work
would put all in good trim. A salt wind came
down the coast. He threw off his cloak and set to.

Nothing but hunger would have stopped him, but
after a while he grew faint, what with the unac-
customed toil and a light breakfast. He would
get his lunch, and when Circe had finished with the
dishes, no doubt she'd like to return with him and
inspect the skiff in which he had voyaged from
fame to fame. She could watch him put on the last
repairs.

On the way to the house he encountered, to his amazement, the original dog, lying by the path and surveying him with skeptical interest, as on the day of his arrival. He was prepared to see the stag again. When he reached the door-step, he noticed a large package on the porch, carefully wrapped and tied. In itself an innocent thing—but he had a mind to peek through the window before venturing inside. In fact, he was stepping carefully through the flower-beds when Circe came out, her most radiant self, charmingly gowned, and the two hounds guarding her.

"Awfully sorry to be late for lunch——"

"Don't mention it," she said. "Your lunch is ready. I've wrapped it up for you."

Puzzled, he looked down at the large package.

"It's food for the voyage," she said. "You can fetch the water yourself from the well."

He looked up for an explanation, but she didn't smile at him—she only looked mildly curious, not deeply impressed—in other words, as he had first seen her.

"A messenger has just come to me," she said, "disguised as a young man."

[125]

"From where?"

"Oh, from heaven, or from providence, or whatever you call it. I have just learned that it is now your fate to move on."

"Has the messenger a light mustache?"

"He has, and a long sword."

Odysseus looked past her into the dining-room, and saw the youth who had warned him, now sitting at table and consuming excellent food. He looked again at Circe, and then he considered the package at his feet.

"If it is my fate, I suppose I might as well go."

He picked up the bundle, and noted with satisfaction that it was heavy. Balancing it on his shoulder, he turned for farewell.

"Since we must part," he said, "thank heaven it's at the moment when our devotion is at its highest. I hate to have to fasten down a slipping romance. But love like ours, a bloom of the spirit——"

He would have said more, but the young man in the dining-room wanted to know why there wasn't salt on the table, and Circe went in to get it for him.

[126]

PART FOUR

THE SIRENS

PART FOUR

THE SIRENS

IF THE lunch Circe had put up for him had lasted longer, Odysseus would never have made the acquaintance of the Sirens. Afterward he tried to make himself believe he had stopped to hear their singing, but what he really wanted was food.

Because his own report varied, the reputation of the Sirens has never been satisfactorily established. Homer says there were two of them, dangerous creatures, whose song lured men to death. They gave their performance seated in a pleasant meadow, surrounded with the bones of previous audiences. When Odysseus and his crew came rowing by, the wise hero forbade the sailors to listen—in fact, he stopped their ears with soft wax, so that the enchantment wouldn't distract them. He himself did without the wax, since the Sirens had quite a name in the musical world and he wanted to be able to say he had heard one of their recitals, but in the manner of many another critic he had himself lashed to the mast for fear he might like it.

The discrepancies in this account are obvious. He had left his men with the Lotus-Eaters, no matter how hard he tried to explain their disappearance otherwise. But if they had been still with him, does any one think they would have submitted to that application of soft wax? Homer's story for once overlooks the first principles of human nature. In this instance he probably accepted the word of Odysseus too literally. It's what you'd expect, not from a poet, but from a man who had no ear for music.

The Sirens enjoy another reputation, far more flattering. According to this legend there were three of them, beautiful to look at and admirable, even spiritual, in their behavior. Their names were Ligeia, Leucosia and Parthenope. Their parents were Phorcys, a local sea-god with philandering tendencies, and Terpsichore, one of the Muses who happened to be in the neighborhood.

In youth the girls had Persephone for playmate; the loss of her made them sad. As they grew older they went in for beauty, for eloquence and for music, and they had a vivid apprehension of the future; their artistic temperament went to such a degree of exaggeration that they used to tell one another they couldn't survive if ever a performance of theirs failed to evoke the customary applause. Then Odysseus sailed right by them, apparently indifferent, and in despair they threw themselves into the sea.

This myth is repeated with variations. The three sisters are sometimes described, not as the beautiful women they were, but as monsters, very feminine and alluring as far down as the waist, but with the thighs and legs of carrion birds. They looked better from a short distance, and preferred to be seated when they sang. Here we see the work of some idle and inferior imagination. It is said also that not Odysseus but Orpheus induced the chagrin which drove them to suicide. When the Argonauts were passing in their quest for the golden fleece, the Sirens tried to lure them

[131]

ashore, but Orpheus seized his lyre and gave a rival performance, one of his best, and the three sisters, hearing the fresh voice and the perfect method of the new star, lost heart and retired. Among the passengers at the moment there was an unfortunate fellow named Butes, in the appreciation of art a one-man dog, so to speak; it went against his conscience to enjoy beauty in more than one style. While the competition was going on, he leaned his ear over the rail toward the Sirens, and then the other way toward Orpheus, making up his mind. At the close of the last number he gave his deliberate opinion that Orpheus had more fire, as one expects of youth, but the way he was going at it, his voice wouldn't last; the Sirens had the correct tradition—it showed in their shading. With that he plunged overboard, like an honest man, and tried to swim to where he belonged, but his friends caught him by the heels just in time.

The inferiority of this version is obvious. We are even told that the father of the Sirens was not Phorcys, tidal and salty, ardent and overwhelming, but Achelous, a fresh-water divinity, slippery and smooth, the slave of gravitation. Absurd!

Leaving Orpheus out of the legend, some of the old poets used the Sirens as a charming parable. Beauty, eloquence and music prosper only so long as they meet a sympathetic eye or a willing ear. To behold beauty and not appreciate it is to annihilate it. When the Sirens performed for Odysseus and he didn't get a thing out of it, for practical purposes they ceased to exist.

That song they sang, too, which we are told is not beyond conjecture—the old poets knew that conjecture was the essence of it, a yearning, a reaching up, such as a high sea utters in its moaning. The almost intolerable heartache in absolute beauty, the sense of want, of loss, of separation, is hidden in the voice of great waters and in the thought of death. Every lovely thing whispers of youth snatched from us. The song of the Sirens, then and now, has in it the remembrance of Persephone.

But what Odysseus was after was food. He

came rowing along the coast, in a bad temper, just as Ligeia, having enjoyed her morning bath, was picking pebbles out of the wet sand. He hoped it might be clams. She stood up straight and watched him. Without further urging he ran the boat ashore, pulled it well up, hitched the anchor to a convenient rock and waited for her to approach.

She came toward him slowly, carrying the pebbles in one hand. Her eyes and her hair were dark, and her olive skin amazingly clear. Long lashes made her face dreamy, she moved erect, the folds of her white garment clung to her, she looked like a sweet goddess painted reverently on an old vase. But not to Odysseus. What he saw was an indolent and exasperating female whose outstretched hand offered for breakfast an assortment of stones.

"If that's your attitude," he said, "I'll move on. I know when I'm not wanted, as well as the next man."

"If you leave so soon," said Ligeia, "we'll always wonder why you stopped at all. Not that we wish to detain you, of course. Are you going anywhere in particular, or are you just rowing around?"

"I'm trying to get home. My wife is waiting for me and I'm late."

"Poor man!" said Ligeia. "With this tide you can't make the mainland before evening. You must rest with us till after lunch."

The word cheered him. "What time is it now?"

"I've lost track," said Ligeia. "I've been swimming. We had breakfast about two hours ago."

"Ah," said the hero. "I'm late."

"Not at all—you're welcome at any time."

They walked up the bank and across the meadow to a small low house, covered on the outside with a reddish earth. There was a roof on it, still redder. In the sunlight the effect was brilliant. Odysseus noted that it was hard on the eyes—the dark stones of Ithaca were in better taste. But he had some curiosity as to what would be found inside. A rather spacious room, with three chairs in it and a table. At least, that was all she showed him. He drew one of the chairs up to the table and sat down. Ligeia took a chair opposite.

[135]

"My sisters are out somewhere," she said. "They'll be back shortly."

"Ah, you have sisters! How many?"

"Just two."

"Well, that's enough," said Odysseus. "And how many brothers?"

"No brothers."

"That's unfortunate. Did they die, or weren't they born?"

"I never had any," said Ligeia.

"Your parents, I suppose, are living with you?"

"No—there's just the three of us."

The mild light in the cool room made her look, as she sat there, like an exquisite goddess carved, perhaps, in a cameo, so clearly the beautiful head was outlined against the shadowy wall. Odysseus was wondering whether it was the absent sisters who did the cooking.

"I dare say you come of a gifted family," he said. "What's your special talent?"

Ligeia smiled. "Nothing. I just am."

"Well," he said, willing to please, "I suppose there's an art in that too. How do your sisters pass the time?"

"Leucosia talks, and Parthenope sings."

"She talks, does she? Don't you all talk?"

"Not the way she does. She has a gift."

"That's very interesting," said Odysseus. He looked bored.

"If eloquence doesn't appeal to you," said Ligeia, "Parthenope sings."

"I heard you say so," said Odysseus. "Who tends to the housekeeping?"

Ligeia laughed. "Well, you know how it is with artists. The housekeeping more or less tends to itself."

"It's a miracle to me," said the hero, "that any artists ever survive."

"Oh, I don't know. Most people put too much thought on things, mere things—furniture, decorations, trimmings, clothes. In comparison with life, such matters are unimportant. And most people eat too much." She sat up straight, and Odysseus, if he cared to, might have noticed what dieting had accomplished for her graceful figure. He didn't notice.

A social instinct aroused him from his meditations.

"I ought to tell you who I am," he said. "It's really too good of you to take me in this way, a total stranger."

"Not at all," said Ligeia. "There's somebody stopping here almost daily. We'd miss it if it didn't happen."

The woman seemed to have no curiosity—no hunger for anything. He thought less of her, but kept on.

"I've just come from Troy."

"Yes?" Ligeia wasn't excited over the news. "They've been having a war there, or something, haven't they?"

"A very notable war," said Odysseus. "You've no doubt heard of it."

"Nothing specific about this one," said Ligeia, "but they're always in trouble out there. Too many brigands and pirates in that part of the world."

"No pirates were involved in this siege." Odysseus was a little stiff. "This war was for a principle—that's why it attracts attention among the thoughtful and well-informed. The question was

[138]

whether the ritual of hospitality should be prac-
tised exclusively in the interest of the guest, or
whether the host, in receiving a stranger, may
retain any property rights. It's a legal point."

"If they fought over that," said Ligeia, "they
must have been hard up for a cause. To think
that men will kill one another for a hypothetical
question!"

"Oh, not hypothetical! The principle which I
have stated in such general terms was embodied
most specifically in Helen. You've heard of her."

"I have not," said Ligeia. "Who is she?"

"Why, she's the most beautiful woman in the
world!"

"Really?" Ligeia was a little stiff.

Odysseus didn't notice it.

"She certainly is. Paris came to visit her husband, and Menelaos received him with scrupulous
correctness—that is beyond dispute—gave him
food at once when he arrived, and the usual number of handsome presents when he left—two or
three admirable vases, a gold-handled but imprac-
tical sword, testimonial of affection from the city

[139]

council of Sparta, and other historic odds and ends such as one reserves for the transient visitor. But when Paris was gone, it was found that he had taken Helen with him. What's worse, she wouldn't come back, and the Trojans wouldn't give her up. So we had to fight it out."

"How silly!" said Ligeia.

"Not silly at all! If a wife can do a thing like that, what becomes of the home?"

"The home seems to have moved to Troy," said Ligeia. "It must have been difficult to punish the most beautiful woman in the world. What did you do to her?"

"Menelaos took her with him."

"He what?"

"Took her back to Sparta. They're probably home by now."

"How absurd!" said Ligeia. "It sounds like a toy war, a game."

"There you're wrong! It was a fierce struggle, for ten years. I really think the Greek force was as well trained and as well equipped as ever took the field. Perhaps you might criticize their high command—there were two opinions as to that. And the Trojans were good too—with certain stimulating advantages; they had strong walls, and Helen to look at. It really was a stand-off."

"I suppose they're still at it," said Ligeia.

Odysseus felt sorry for her.

"No, the war came to an end some years ago——"

"Years ago?"

"That's what I said. One of the ablest of the Greeks, perhaps the ablest, invented the wooden horse."

Ligeia laughed outright. It occurred to him that she might be half-witted. That would explain the housekeeping.

"Yes, the wooden horse—an immense effigy, big enough to hold a number of Greeks. The Trojans drew the thing inside their walls, and after dark the concealed warriors came out, opened the gates to their comrades and destroyed the town."

"I never heard anything more delightful," said Ligeia. "You must meet my sister Leucosia—she's the story-teller of the family. She'll adore this

[141]

one. But she's a severe critic. I foresee she'll pounce on one or two discrepancies."

"Which?"

"Well, suppose the Trojans hadn't pulled the horse inside the walls? How could you go on from there? You'll admit they were extremely obliging. But perhaps you can mend that place before she comes in."

"My dear young woman," said Odysseus, "this isn't a literary effort—this really happened! They *did* take in the horse!"

For a moment she looked a bit frightened, then she became conciliatory.

"Of course they did! You know, because you were there. Of course! It must have been fascinating to watch."

"Good heavens!" said Odysseus. "I never had harder work articulating a plain fact. I didn't look on—I was in it!"

"In the horse?"

"Certainly!"

A wave of pity made her eyes unusually tender, and she answered him gently.

"How stupid I am! No doubt you were the clever Greek who invented the machine."

"Now you've got it!" said Odysseus. "That's who I was."

She gazed at him quite a while, then slowly shook her head.

"Wonderful!" she said. . . . "Wonderful!"

She got up and went to the doorway. "I can't imagine what's keeping my sisters. Do you mind if I go look for them?"

"Perhaps you'd better," said the hero. "Clearly they've been detained. I'll amuse myself—don't have me on your mind."

In fact, he had some curiosity to explore the house. When she was safely started he opened the door into the living quarters. Nothing there to indicate what these women really were. . . . Three tiny rooms, no bigger than cells . . . a bed in each, the plainest kind of bed . . . he tried one—very hard . . . no hooks to hang clothes on . . . in fact, no clothes. . . . What sort of people were these? They owned nothing but what was on their backs! For absolute poverty,

[143]

disguised in culture, he had never met such a case. The house had promised well, from the outside.

He returned to the deserted living-room, sat down at the table once more, and tried to think it over. Perhaps this girl wasn't so innocent nor so ignorant as she appeared. Perhaps she had known from the first who he was. How did it happen she was on the beach just as he came along? And her sisters out for a walk? . . . What if she had acted the part of a decoy? This queer house might be a trap! She'd be coming in any minute now, perhaps, with those mythical sisters, who would turn out to be brothers, pirates, robbers! Hadn't she mentioned pirates? If he only had a knife!

Or maybe the woman was crazy. The way she saw something funny about the wooden horse! Her family perhaps kept her here for safety, and emptied the house so she wouldn't have anything to hurt herself with. In that case, in any case, he'd better move on before she returned.

But, crazy or not, pirate or honest, the woman must have some food stored somewhere. . . . He examined the rooms again, and found a little door he had overlooked, out of one of the cells. Locked, of course. He put his shoulder against it and broke in. Ah! The pantry! Tidy shelves, with a number of enticing jars on them—nine, to be precise. If he took with him the most suitable, and closed the door carefully behind him, that lunatic would never notice the difference. Now for jar number one! . . . It was empty. So was number two . . . and number three . . . and four . . . empty, and washed clean as a whistle! At number eight he was so exasperated that he threw the vessel on the floor. It smashed with a horrible noise. Served it right! . . . But number nine—ah, number nine was full of succulent beans!

He had just made the discovery when he heard voices outside the house. Women. He held his breath. The men might be with them. What a place to be caught in!

"I'm *sure* I heard something break, just a moment ago! Perhaps he is violent!"

"Nonsense!" He recognized Ligeia's intonation. "He's as harmless as a child."

"Well," said a third voice, "I'd like to go in first, if you don't mind. I think I can manage him best alone. Wait outside, and if anything goes wrong, I'll call. Isn't it lucky I found the ax!"

It occurred to Odysseus that he ought to receive them in the large room. Food or no food! He was so hasty with the precious jar that he didn't get it back squarely on the shelf. When it hit the floor it made more noise than number eight, and a tide of beans flooded him up to the ankles. As he went out he slammed the pantry door. He was just emerging from the sleeping quarters, at high speed, when a rather thick-set woman came in the main entrance. She had dark hair, like Ligeia, but her eyes were blue and her skin less ethereal. Her shoulders were broad and her chest extraordinarily developed—that is, suggesting lung power rather than charm. An efficient woman. She betrayed no surprise at the place she found him in—she looked as though guests always dashed out of the bedroom.

"Ah, there you are!" She had a lovely voice, resonant and velvety, but in the hurry of the moment he missed its quality. "Now suppose we sit here at the table and have a quiet talk. My name is Leucosia. My sister says that you were at Troy some years ago, in one of the most notable wars. How enchanting! I'd love to hear about it. And you fought for a principle. How noble of you, really! And for a woman at the same time. How unusual! Quite the most beautiful woman who ever lived. Ligeia says it's incredible, but the audacity of the theme appeals to me. It's a subject for poetry. Helen . . . that was the name? Helen! How easy to pronounce! The very sound evokes beauty. That's what I always say—there's nothing like liquids to help out a word. Helen! You see? The 'l' and the 'n.' Perfect! Of course you must think of her as beautiful, with a name like that!"

He was about to say that Helen was good to look at, no matter what her name made you think of, but Leucosia didn't pause long enough for him to get started.

"My sister says you were the leader of the Greek forces. She didn't catch the name."

[147]

"I doubt if I told her," said Odysseus. "As a matter of fact, the leader of the expedition was Agamemnon."

"That's a good name too," said Leucosia. "Liquids again, you observe. You must be proud of it."

"I'm not. It isn't my name. I am Odysseus."

"Will you pronounce it again, more slowly?"

"Odysseus!"

"How odd! Odysseus! Hm! Preponderance of sibilants!"

So she was crazy too. The whole family.

"If I'm not mistaken," he said, "there's some one outside your door."

"Oh, is there? Perhaps it's my sisters. Come in! It's all right!"

Ligeia came in at once, followed by a tall thin girl whose eyes were dark but her hair quite golden.

"You've met Ligeia, I believe—this is Parthenope."

There were only three chairs. Ligeia sat gracefully on the edge of the table.

"Our visitor—there, that name's gone again!"

"Odysseus."

"Of course! He was telling me about Troy and Helen, and what he's been doing since. Or he was about to when you came in."

"I hadn't said a thing."

"But you will now, won't you? How have you been managing all these years, in a little boat?"

"When I left Troy I had a ship."

"And you lost it somewhere? You poor man! What was the matter with it?"

He foresaw embarrassment if he told the truth about the Lotus episode. They wouldn't admire him for leaving his men in the lurch—that is, if he told the story that way—and much less if he confessed that he was put out but they were allowed to remain.

"My ship was wrecked in a bad storm just after I left Circe's island. I've been staying with Circe."

"Did your men go down with the ship?" said Leucosia.

"Every last one of them."

"And where did you get the small boat you came in?"

There! He knew he was going to overlook something!

[149]

"As a matter of fact, the boat was little short of a miracle. After the ship foundered, I swam around in a hopeless sort of way—it happened at night, in a wild storm—any minute I thought would be my last. Suddenly I collided with something hard. It must have stunned me—I believe I lost consciousness—when I came to, I was clinging to the side of the boat. One can do that by instinct. I climbed in and started to row."

Leucosia had a hard eye on him.

"None of your men could swim? Didn't you rescue any of them?"

"Why, certainly. I did my best. That is, I rowed backward and forward over the spot, and called from time to time, but no one answered. They must have sunk like rocks."

"If I were telling the incident," said Leucosia, "I'd be tempted to say that while you were unconscious the wind and the tide bore you far away, so that when you tried to find them it was too late."

"Very probably," said Odysseus.

"And from my point of view the men must have

been cursed. A wholesale disaster of that kind implies some hidden wickedness. Weren't they guilty of some sin which needed retribution?"

"Undoubtedly they were—it's not for me to say which particular sin."

"If you tell the story at all, you ought to be specific," said Leucosia. "If you don't give a reason for things, a story is no better than life."

"I'm not trying to make up a yarn. Life is good enough for me. I'm telling the truth."

"What happened to you on Circe's island?"

"I stayed there a year. You've heard of her, perhaps?"

"All about her. What did she do to you?"

"A very delightful woman," he said. "I—I may say I loved her."

"Of course—every one does. How did she behave about it?"

"It sounds rather flat to mention it myself—but she loved me too."

"I can understand that," said Leucosia. He didn't see her wink at her sisters. "Did she work any of her magic on you?"

"She tried to, but I was warned in advance. It didn't take."

"That's why you left, I suppose?"

"No—she had instructions from a god to permit me to resume my journey. You see, I'm on my way home. In Ithaca at this moment my wife Penelope is grieving. Perhaps she thinks I'm dead."

"That explains it," said Leucosia. "Naturally when you're in a hurry like that, you can't stay with Circe more than a year. What were your men doing all the while?"

Confound it! He had forgotten the men. He fought for time.

"The crew of my ship? They were with me— the ship hadn't yet gone down, you know."

"Yes, but how did they amuse themselves? Wasn't Circe interested in them too?"

Ah, happy thought! "She turned them into pigs."

The three sisters gave an exclamation, and Leucosia laughed outright.

"I never should have thought of that," she said.

"Yes, they went ashore first, looking for fresh

water, and she put the magic on them. I found them in her pigsty. Of course I made her restore them to their usual shape."

"You did that at once, of course?"

"I didn't lose a day."

Leucosia reflected.

"And then you fell in love with her. That shows how difficult it is to know in advance what a man admires in a woman. I should have thought you would have stayed just long enough to get the sailors out of her clutches. The love-making would perhaps be an attempt to wheedle the secret out of her. That would take months, with a witch so clever. Then in a melting moment, as she expired in your arms, she would whisper the formula, you would set the men free, and leave her weeping on the shore, tearing her hair, you know, and all that."

"Now that you recall it to my memory——" said Odysseus.

"I thought it happened that way," said Leucosia. "What adventure did you have before Circe?"

The sweat stood on his brow. Hunger made him

[153]

faint, and the woman's cross-examination drove him frantic. He resolved to leave at the first pause in the talk.

"I stayed with the Lotus-Eaters a few days," he said. "Nothing worth mentioning."

"Did you enjoy eating Lotus?"

"No, but it's better than nothing. It's a kind of bread, made without salt or other flavoring. They don't cook it enough, either. No, I shan't try to introduce it at home."

"While you were eating this bread," said Leucosia, "what did your men do?"

"The same thing," said Odysseus. "They liked it. You see, there's a sort of magic in the stuff— once you begin, you can't stop. They would have been eating there still, and making love to the native girls, if I hadn't led them forcibly to the ship. It was one of those cases where a leader has to be rough for the good of his men."

Leucosia caught him again.

"Why didn't the magic work on you?"

"Oh, I was careful not to eat. I was warned in advance."

[154]

"But you said you did eat—you told us what it tasted like."

"I beg pardon—you must have misunderstood me." He turned to the sisters. "Did you gather that I too ate?"

"You made it very clear," said Ligeia.

"It must have been a slip of the tongue. No, I was on my guard."

"How about those native women," said Leucosia. "I suppose you had to be on your guard there?"

"I couldn't relax my vigilance a moment."

All three looked at him in silence. His gaze was fixed on his feet. On the top of the left shoe he observed a large bean.

"I think I'll move on now," he said. "Thanks for the hospitality!"

"Oh, we forgot all about lunch!" said Ligeia, making for the door of the pantry.

"Not for me!" said Odysseus. "I couldn't eat a thing."

"Get him that jar of beans," said Parthenope. "If he isn't hungry now, he can eat them later in his boat."

"Thanks a lot," said Odysseus, "but beans I never under any circumstances eat."

Ligeia hesitated at the pantry door.

"If you would all walk down to the boat and see me off, it would be a gesture of hospitality much appreciated in my country."

As they went out, he noticed a bright ax leaning against the house.

"But I'm embarrassed that we didn't feed you," said Ligeia. They were already on their way to the shore. "Let me run back and fetch the jar!"

"I couldn't think of it. You've provided me with an hour's rest and with some helpful ideas."

"Tell me one thing," said Ligeia. "Who decided that Helen is the most beautiful woman?"

"I've heard of one man who doubted it. He was born blind, and he loved to argue."

"She must be lovely," said Ligeia, "but how can you be sure she excels till you've seen all the other women in the world?"

"I've seen most of them," said Odysseus, "and it looks as though I'd meet the others before I got home. She's in a class by herself."

[156]

He didn't see why the silence, as they walked on, should be so awkward.

"In our family," said Parthenope at last, "we've always thought Ligeia good-looking."

"Natural enough," said Odysseus, without raising his eyes from the path.

They continued without further words.

Half-way to the boat Ligeia said she was tired and would wait there for her sisters.

"Good-by," said Odysseus. "If ever you're in the neighborhood of Ithaca, we'll hope to see you." She sat down on a smooth rock, and he went on with the other two.

"The next time you tell those interesting experiences of yours," said Leucosia, "remember the suggestions I gave you. You do remarkably well for a novice, but you want to look out for those crude gaps. The whole art is to keep the critical faculties of your hearers in a state of somnolence. Once they begin to question the details, you might as well stop."

"What do you mean by novice?" said Odysseus. "This Troy affair has occupied the prime of my life. You talk as though I were a weak-minded minstrel. I *lived* all this, I tell you! Sometimes I forget a fact here and there, but in the main I report the simple truth. The trouble with you is, you're too theoretical. As a woman, shut up here on this desert island, you haven't had a fair chance at experience, and I suppose solitude and common sense don't grow together. Men and women are art enough for me. If you want to know how to tell a story, get into the next war, as a captive or any way you like. You'll find that your memory afterward will be full of crude gaps."

Leucosia didn't answer. She walked on a hundred yards or so, and then held out her hand.

"I'm tired too," she said. "I'll wait for Parthenope here."

Odysseus was too hungry and too irritable to use all his best manners.

"All right," he said. "Good-by."

He and Parthenope were soon out of earshot.

"In our family," she said, "we've always thought Leucosia had a great talent for story-telling, for the enchantment of language."

[158]

"So?" said Odysseus. "She evidently has a marked interest, but that's not enough to constitute a talent."

Again they moved in silence.

"What's your gift supposed to be?"

"I sing a little," she said.

"Well, there's no harm in that. Music's all right if you don't give your whole time to it. Who'd you study with?"

"Oh, I taught myself."

"Hm!" said Odysseus. Not another word till they came to the shore.

"By the way, do you know what direction Troy is from here?"

"No. I'm sorry."

"It doesn't matter. I'll ask as I go along."

Parthenope seated herself where the meadow met the sand, and Odysseus got the boat ready. The tide was out, and he'd have to drag the thing twenty feet or more. He got the anchor loose from the rock, stowed the rope, inspected the oarlocks, examined the water supply.

"You don't happen to have a well, do you?"

[159]

"Oh, yes, in the next field. I'll show you."

She led the way and he followed with the empty goatskin under his arm. When the water was in it, he got it up on his shoulder and staggered back toward the shore. As she walked Parthenope was swinging her arms. The rhythm suggested song. She began to sing. Really a marvelous voice. And the song would drag your heart out—if you weren't hungry.

"Do you happen to know," said Odysseus, "what island comes next if I keep straight ahead?"

"I don't. I'm sorry." She began again, this time to herself, softly. An extraordinary *mezzo voce*, a vibrant whisper, a breath, a yearning.

"I should think you and your sisters would be lonely here," said Odysseus. "Leucosia needs experience if she is going to dabble in story-telling, but all of you, as human beings, ought to get out of this rut. I always say a man or a woman is entitled to at least as much experience as caused him to be born. Otherwise there would be a sad shrinkage from generation to generation."

"That's not clear," said Parthenope, "or perhaps

[160]

I didn't hear correctly. I was singing when you spoke."

"My thought was simplicity itself," he said. "If your parents hadn't married or at least fallen in love with each other, you wouldn't be here. You're therefore entitled to a lover."

"Many men stop here," she said. "We're not so isolated as you think. If a great man should ever arrive, I dare say one of us might lose her heart. Of course there ought to be three great men. Leucosia says it's asking too much of life. We're quite happy with our fate. We are wedded to our art."

"Your art?"

"We are lovers of ideal beauty, I think. It's the family temperament."

"I've heard of it," said the hero. "It won't get you anywhere. It may prevent you from recognizing a great man when you see one."

Parthenope laughed. "Don't worry about us. We'll make no mistake."

He disliked her exceedingly. That horribly penetrating voice, those conceited airs! He wished

[161]

she wouldn't hum under her breath while he was talking.

Again she sat down at the edge of the meadow. He put the water-skin in the boat and tried to launch it. It wouldn't budge. Another attempt. He thought the muscles would pull out of his arms. Evidently the boat was there to stay.

"Why don't you take out the water and any other heavy thing in it, and move the boat empty?"

He didn't care for advice from her, but the idea was sound. He carried the baggage and the oars to the edge of the sea, and tugged again. The boat moved three inches. Once more! Three inches at a time. He reduced it to a system, a regular pull, like the swing of a pendulum. At this rate, if he didn't faint with hunger, he'd be launched in half an hour. Those crazy sisters had something to answer for! With the normal amount of food in him he could have handled the boat in no time.

Parthenope, deeply interested in his heaving, began to sing, following the beat, as it were.

"Would you mind stopping that noise?" he shouted.

She stopped at once. She rose gracefully and walked back toward the house.

His own rudeness made him more than ever irritable. By the time the boat was afloat and the baggage in place again, he was in a nervous fury. He pulled straight out to sea. The red roof of the house showed above the shore. He could watch that white figure walking away. No, it was running toward him. It wasn't Parthenope, it was Ligeia. She was waving the largest fragment of the shattered bean jar. At the beach she put a hand to her mouth and shrieked at him. He stopped rowing then.

"What—did—you—do—to—the—beans?"

He stood up in the boat and put both hands to his lips.

"What—did—you—do—with—the—bones?"

She couldn't understand.

"Bones—the—bones—of—your—visitors?"

Now she put her hand to her ear. He sat down again at the oars, backed the boat in a way, and tried again.

"Do—you—bury—them—or—do—they—always—leave—before—they—die?" the hero shouted.

She shook her head in despair.

"Damned harpy!" said Odysseus to himself. "Now what comes next?"

PART FIVE

CALYPSO

PART FIVE

CALYPSO

WHEN the wind freshened he put up his sail. Without food he could row no longer. The wind was steady enough for all purposes, if he had had his wits about him, and the first part of the night passed without accident. Then he fell asleep with the sail drawing full and his hand on the tiller.

He had a remarkable dream, in which the Ciconian woman, Daphne and Parthenope were entangled. He thought he was falling, ever so slowly, from a great height. Sometimes it was down that hill, escaping not nearly fast enough from the fatal palace and the new grave, and sometimes he was diving off the rock with Daphne. She didn't care now whether or not he was a king—there was a tender, not to say proprietary look in her eyes, and as they disappeared beneath the wave her arms

[167]

were around him. He wished she would let go, so that he might swim, but she held on. She whispered in his ear. If he understood her in-delicate communication, she was notifying him that now she must have that long-desired child. It made him laugh, even in that plight, to observe what thoughts a drowning woman can carry to the bottom of the ocean. Suddenly he decided he'd rather not drown. What would Penelope do without him? He began to fight for his life, but the woman was outrageously strong. Ah, he might have known— it wasn't Daphne, it was that Ciconian girl. What one would expect of her! If he could pull one arm loose, perhaps he could choke her before the last of his breath was gone. But when he pulled, the expression on her face changed, and an un-pleasant noise started in his ears. Parthenope! He resigned himself to drowning. . . . The mo-ment he relaxed, he woke up wet and cold, sousing in the water alongside his overturned boat.

It was pitch dark. The stars were out, but they didn't seem to do any good. He pulled himself around to the stern and climbed up on the keel.

The night air on his wet clothes was chilly. He foresaw he might fall asleep again any moment, and the next time perhaps he'd drown. No, probably not. The water was comfortably smooth, and if he fell in he'd wake up. He stretched himself along the keel and let fate do what it would.

It was early morning when he came to. The wind had disappeared altogether, and only a slow mysterious current moved the steady boat. He was passing an island, an attractive cluster of trees, with one gentle hill rising out of them, and a hospitable shore. He tried to paddle the boat with his feet, but the sail underneath anchored it in the stream. He'd be far beyond the island before he could set the mass in motion. Well, the first heavy wind would lift him off the slippery keel—it was land or nothing. He got rid of his remaining rags and swam ashore.

Calypso was at her loom, in the door of her cave, singing as she walked to and fro with the shuttle in her hand. He had never heard a pleasanter voice. It suggested motherliness and a good breakfast. Before a less wonderful woman he would

[169]

have been embarrassed by his informal appearance, but something in Calypso's voice told him she'd hardly notice the difference. He walked right up to her.

She was a large female, beautifully proportioned. That impression came first. A tall substantial woman with a generous mouth, a cordial smile, big brown eyes set wide apart, and rich auburn hair done up in massive braids. They fell over her shoulders down to her knees. She seemed neither surprised nor offended.

"My dear man! What on earth has happened to you?"

The immediate intimacy suggested the fear that she mistook him for an old friend.

"Madam, I am an unfortunate stranger who has no right to intrude, but having just escaped drowning I wonder if with your assistance I may now escape starvation."

"You won't have to ask that question twice," said the divine creature. "Do you prefer to dress before breakfast or afterward?"

"If it's ready now," said Odysseus, "and if

[170]

you'll overlook the impropriety, I'll sit down as I am."

It was an honest meal, warm and savory, and she had the sense not to ask a question till he was fed. He remembered, by way of contrast, Circe and her niggardly manners.

"You have my gratitude for ever, madam. You've saved my life."

Calypso leaned across the table toward him, with her chin in her hands, and gazed deep into his eyes.

"You may have saved mine," she said. "Who knows? Just this morning I was hoping for some break in this lonely existence, for some one to share the wasted plenty of this isle. I knew no one would ever come—yet here you are! You won't think me overbold—you're too intelligent a man—but I'm glad to see you."

"I suppose I ought to dress," he said, "but I'm too lazy to move."

"Let me suggest the program," said Calypso. "If you've been shipwrecked you're probably sleepy as well as famished. Let's talk a while, till you feel like a nap—then I'll find you a soft bed and a warm blanket, and when you wake we'll see what there is in the way of clothes."

She was neither too forward nor too reticent, neither lacking in initiative nor domineering. A perfect woman, he could see that. Why hadn't he got there sooner?

"I like to talk," he said, "with a woman who has brains. You're the first I've met."

"Ever?" said Calypso.

"I had in mind the present voyage," said Odysseus, "but it's true in the large. Yes, the first brainy one I ever met."

"You're married, I take it."

"Why do you say that?"

"Husbands are severe critics. Wives are too. I'm not married myself."

"You certainly have a delightful disposition," said Odysseus, "and in other ways also you've no doubt done better without one of my sex to work for and worry over. My wife's an admirable woman, extremely skilful in administration. You never saw such a housekeeper. I'm yearning to see her again, of course, but when I get there I hope I may arrive with my clothes on and in good order. She's that kind. Now you, I can see, take a liberal view. You like everything as it should be, but you aren't blind to the element of chance in the universe, you have a merciful sense of humor, and a palate for the flavors of life—what they call gusto. You're to be congratulated—and since I arrived here, thanks to the gods, I'm to be envied."

He hadn't been so set up in years. Nor had Calypso.

"Who are you?" she said. "I know you're a great man, but I can't guess which one."

"I am Odysseus," he said as modestly as possible.

"You don't mean you're the king of Ithaca? Not the famous orator? Not the genius who brought the war to a close?"

Joy made her hysterical. He thought best simply to nod his head.

"To think that you are sitting at my table!"

Really, her ecstasy was embarrassing.

"I marvel that you have heard of me, madam, in this remote island."

"Ah, but who hasn't heard, everywhere? You're on your way home now? How glad Penelope will be to see you! I can imagine her emotions!"

"I hope she'll be glad," said Odysseus. "I used to be able to imagine her sentiments, but time works many changes. The nearer I get to my domicile the more I approach it with curiosity." Never before had he confessed to such an impersonal attitude.

"You don't have to hurry, do you? If she's waited so long, a few days more won't matter, and at this stage in your weary voyage you ought to rest, get yourself into first-rate condition."

"My nervous system is depleted," said Odysseus. "Madam, if you knew——"

"Let's drop ceremony—call me Calypso!"

"With pleasure! As I was saying, if you knew what I've been suffering——"

"Do tell me! You'd be sure to have wonderful adventures—I can see you have the gift for finding them out. Wherever you stopped, some woman now has an aching heart."

"Well, of course," said the hero, "I'm not the

one to confirm your guess. I *have* met several interesting women——"

"Begin at the beginning," said Calypso.

"When my men and I sailed away from Troy——"

"Where are your men now?"

Thanks to Leucosia, he was ready for her.

"Several nights ago, in the storm which reduced me to this nakedness, but which gave me the pleasure of your society, my ship was struck by lightning, and, except for myself, every soul was drowned. If you were of a critical disposition, which fortunately you aren't, you might now ask me how I could be so cheerful, having sustained the loss of so many friends. The fact is, they had ceased to be my friends. Perhaps their virtue was exhausted by wanderings too protracted, but they indulged in forms of wickedness which I couldn't name to a woman. I did my best to save their souls—warned them, threatened them, preached at them, prayed over them, set them a good example—but they persisted. Sooner or later heaven had to blast the outfit. I grieve inwardly, but it's a mis-

[175]

take to let the errors of your fellow man cloud your life."

Calypso reached across the table and squeezed his hand.

"Well, to go back—when we sailed from Troy we came first to the land of the Ciconians, an aggressive, hostile people. There was a sharp fight, I regret to say. As soon as we had taken the city, I ordered my men at once to the ship—we couldn't be sure the neighboring tribes wouldn't come down on us. But some of my men—you'll forgive this gross detail—had captured the native women, and I might just as well have given no orders at all. The neighboring tribes *did* arrive. I nearly lost my life rescuing those low-minded sailors."

"It must be twice as hard," said Calypso, "to incur danger when it's to help out those who don't deserve it. How generous you were! And I dare say the sailors were drunk. Those native women are unattractive."

"Oh, there was one girl——" The memory of Leucosia warned him against so bad a start. "But I shan't offend you with her story."

[176]

"She was handsome?"

"In a sense, but she lacked the instinct of modesty. After the Ciconians we visited the Lotus-Eaters, with the same general results, except that there was no fight. They live on a queer bread, which steals away your mind. Of course I was careful to avoid it, myself, but the men were imprudent, as usual. I had to drive them by force back to the ship. A few, in fact, declined to be driven. At this moment they are probably eating away. Their wives and children wait for them in vain."

Calypso dried a tear. "The Lotus women are beautiful, aren't they?"

He pursed his lips and racked his memory.

"I don't know that you'd say so. They have a misleading air of innocence about them—many of the sailors succumbed. I had an odd encounter myself—not the sort of thing I could tell every one, but you will understand. There was one girl there, rather refined in appearance, who attached herself to me. If you'll believe it, I'd hardly met her when she asked me to give her a child! Forgive my

[177]

mentioning it! Poor thing, her thoughts ran rather too much on that subject, and she wasn't responsible."

"I hope," said Calypso, "you did what she asked?"

"No. I'm not a prude, but the conditions weren't just right. With my men looking to me for guidance—you understand."

"I didn't believe a man could be so noble!"

"Oh, I don't call it noble. Prudent, perhaps. Well, then we landed on Circe's island."

"You don't mean it? How did you get free?"

"It wasn't easy. My men went ashore first, looking for fresh water, and she turned them into animals. To be specific, pigs. The insult was studied. She had put an enchanted poison in their food. When I realized their predicament, I went at once to her house and demanded their release. It took a year to persuade her. A terrible experience."

"How did you persuade her?"

Odysseus paused and considered the next step. Perhaps frankness would be best—that is, within reason.

[178]

"I just told you, I'm not a prude. Circe made some plain proposals to me, the moment we met— I might as well have stayed among the Lotus-Eaters. Viewing the matter in the large, I thought I ought to think first of my unfortunate men, at whatever cost to my sensibilities. I made their release the price of my—of my—well, concession. Circe was stubborn, but I was a little more so. At the end of the year she gave in, I kept my word, and we came on away."

"Never have I heard such a heroic story!" said Calypso. "You were so clever to avoid the enchanted poison."

"Well, I was beginning to have a good deal of experience by that time. I carried food from the ship, something I could rely on. The men wouldn't take that simple precaution."

"And from there you came to me?"

"No, from there we visited the Sirens. I mean, we passed them. A bad lot, those three. Two of them, anyway."

"One of them sings well, I understand," said Calypso.

[179]

"It's as you happen to feel about it," said Odysseus. "I was taking no chances. My men wanted to stop there for food and water—they'd heard about the singing, too. I took precautions."

"Which?"

"I didn't stop."

"Oh, you should have! One of them's famous for her beauty. At least you could have heard them sing. Or you could have put wax in your ears, and just looked at them."

"I wish I *had* had wax in my ears!"

"Or," said Calypso, "if you had wanted to listen in safety, you could have put the wax in the sailors' ears, and they would have rowed you by, whether or not you thought of landing."

Odysseus made a note of this embellishment, for future use.

"I got off well. I've no regrets."

Calypso gazed on him in deeper admiration.

"You must know so much! To you, now, I suppose a woman is an open book!"

He shook his head. "I wouldn't say so. To be sure, I've stored up some impressions."

[180]

"Do share them with me!"

"Well, the first that comes to mind may sound uncomplimentary, but it's impersonal. From what I've seen of women I think they're too preoccupied nowadays with sex."

Calypso nodded mournful agreement.

"Sex in a natural way," he went on, "is all right, of course, but this surreptitious hinting about, this inward nursing of the mood, is unhealthy. I'm not vain enough to think they fall in love with me as an individual; they've reached such a state they lose their poise when any sort of person happens along. I can't see what it will all come to."

"There's certainly little reticence left in the world," said Calypso. "Living alone as I do, the problem hardly affects me, but if I had a son or daughter to bring up, I'd worry."

Odysseus looked at her handsome face, her superb body, and he rather envied the possible father of the son and daughter.

"I'm amazed you never married, Calypso. I should have thought your aptitudes were highly domestic."

She toyed with the table-cloth a moment before answering.

"I'll be frank—I wanted a man—I wanted children—but it would have to be the right man, of course, and he never came."

It sounded tragic. The idea induced melancholy. He felt chilly and remembered the promised blanket.

"If you don't mind, I'll sleep a while now," he said. "After I'm rested I can talk much better. You'll pardon my stupid chatter?"

She pardoned it, and showed him to his couch— a gorgeous affair, long enough for a giant, and as broad as it was long. It occurred to him that no other couch was visible—perhaps Calypso was sacrificing her own convenience—but she probably didn't take a nap in the daytime, and later he could arrange a bunk for himself.

She left him, tucked in and cozy. Before she was out of the cave he was lost in dreamless rest.

Just before sunset he woke up. She was busy with the supper, humming to herself as she turned the meat on the fire. He lay still and watched.

[182]

How haunting that song was! And for sheer beauty, the woman was devastating. She had changed her gown. This one was nothing but an exquisite film. Good heavens, the woman had the figure of a goddess! Ligeia? Circe? Daphne? The Ciconian? Helen? Bosh! This woman was unique. He unwrapped himself from the blankets.

"What shall I wear, now I'm up?" he called.

"You'll find one of my dresses over the chair—can you do anything with that?"

He tried hard, but at last he gave it up. It was too roomy, too diaphanous. He thought of hitching it up with a belt, but the result was ludicrous.

"So far as I'm concerned," said Calypso, "nothing is really necessary, provided you're warm enough. You understand I couldn't say that to any one else, but we aren't like ordinary people—you appreciate frankness and common sense. In this sequestered spot the usual conventions lapse. You and I need for guidance only our consciences and our self-respect."

Odysseus folded the gown carefully and laid it over the back of the chair.

[183]

"Can't I help you with the meal? I often do when I'm at home and the servants are out."

She let him help and didn't criticize the results. He sat down to the table a happy man.

"Since we've begun to be frank with each other," he said, "you won't consider it idle flattery if I tell you I've never met a woman so entirely companionable. I was aware of something reassuring in the atmosphere the moment I reached your island. Hitherto I've thought of my wanderings as an affliction. This episode I shall remember in other terms."

"It makes me sad to hear you call it an episode. You're not thinking of leaving already?"

"I've no right to impose on you," said Odysseus, helping himself the second time to a creamy sauce. "It's delightful here, but, after all, you are entitled to your privacy. A sensitive man doesn't care to be an interloper."

"You're not—you never could be. Do stay!"

"It wouldn't be so difficult for me," he went on, "if I could feel I was useful to you, but the house is so admirably organized, a man is superfluous."

[184]

"Well, you needn't decide for a day or two. I'd like you to be strong again and rested before you attempt the sea once more."

Since he had no intention of leaving so long as the table maintained the present standard, he dropped the subject. At the end of the meal he was comfortable in every department of his being. In fact, a little drowsy. They sat watching the last lights flush the fleecy clouds.

"If I'm not mistaken, Calypso, that admirable bedstead is yours. Before it gets too dark I'll knock together half a dozen boards for a bunk. Where shall I locate it?"

"There's no hurry," said Calypso. "After supper I like to talk, and the opportunity comes so seldom."

They sat there in silence. Odysseus managed not to yawn.

"May I speak to you without reserve?" said Calypso. "There's a subject I've been thinking of for several years. . . . Our ideas of marriage, it seems to me, are obsolete. What is your opinion?"

Odysseus roused himself.

"Obsolete? Why, I don't know. . . . Which ideas do you refer to?"

"Let's put it this way," said Calypso. "Men and women marry for the pleasure of their own company, or they wish to have children. That's true, isn't it?"

"That certainly covers two of the cases."

"Well, then. If they marry just for each other, it's no one's business but their own, and we needn't give them another thought. But if they intend to increase the sum total of human beings, the rest of us have the right to demand that the offspring be sound in body and mind, unhandicapped. You agree, I assume?"

"To be entirely frank," said Odysseus, "I've always allowed my neighbors to do what they could. I never made any demands. Perhaps I neglected my duty."

"It's a duty which really begins with ourselves," said Calypso. "That's why I've given the matter so much thought. I have no neighbors. You'll understand me when I say I'm the type of woman nature meant to be a mother. The tragedy of my

[186]

life is that until this minute I've never had a child, nor the slightest prospect of one. How could I? The men I've met were not the sort of ancestors a child would thank you for. In some instances their morals were decidedly suspect. In others, they lacked a satisfactory physique. We'll come to know, some day, that it's not enough for a man to be correct; he must have stamina. I'm not talking too plainly, am I?"

"Not for me," said Odysseus. "Your remarks are most stimulating. Do continue!"

"I've a simple habit of measuring the potential father of my children by myself. My parents endowed me with perfect health, which I have been careful to preserve. I'm conscious of more vitality than seems to animate most people. From time to time a man has dropped in here, and sat in that chair you now occupy, and we've exchanged ideas, but often the visitor misunderstood my thoughts, and companionship was out of the question, or else I suspected that our child would represent only the average of vitality between us, and it would really be too horrible to produce a weakling, even speaking in comparisons. It would be a crime against the race."

Odysseus followed sympathetically.

"I've learned the same thing in Ithaca, raising cattle. No matter how carefully you choose the parents, unless you happen to know their ancestry for years back, you may get a bad surprise."

"I didn't mean it quite that way," said Calypso. "In a few cases I've been able to trace the ancestry of the men I've considered, but when I looked squarely at the men themselves I knew that the past was past. The family had run out."

"Ah yes," said Odysseus, "that's the frequent result of a disordered way of life. I wish our young people could see the profitableness of the old-fashioned virtues. When I get home I hope my son——"

"Then you have a son?" said Calypso. "I wanted to ask."

"Yes, a fine fellow, taller than I am, every inch a man. When I stand between him and my father, I have to admit I bring down the family average."

Calypso returned to her theme. "I shouldn't

have asked any of those men to stay with me for ever, or to give up their careers—it wouldn't be fair. All I wanted was the child. We should be friends afterward, of course, but the father could go where he liked."

"It's a liberal program, far ahead of the times," said Odysseus. "You've had awfully bad luck."

They watched the horizon, now almost dark.

"There's another idea I'd like to speak of. When you came to-day, I thought perhaps you were the man I've been waiting for. I hope you don't think me indelicate? The thought would naturally occur, since the subject has occupied my mind for so many years."

"Nothing could be more natural," said Odysseus, "nor in better taste. You fill me with profound respect."

"The average woman to-day does pay too much attention to sex, as you remarked. I regret to admit it. Flirtation, intrigue, all that sort of thing is foreign to my disposition. Perhaps that's why I never encountered, not till this morning, a man who could see what I was dreaming of. Their training

[189]

had been with the average woman, elusive and indirect. You I knew I could approach with an honest heart."

She paused. He thought he understood her, but the adventure was so novel, he decided to wait till she made a specific suggestion.

"What I should like to say, then, in few words, is to ask you—I'd like to offer—no, that's not it— Odysseus, I want a child, as glorious as you, as full of vitality as I feel, worthy of us both! May I have a child?"

It was as though she had asked him to hand her the sugar. It wouldn't be good table manners to refuse.

He clasped her to him. She was even larger than he had thought. It was his habit, in such cases, to pick the woman bodily from the floor and carry her in his impassioned arms. It always made an effect. He started to try it now, but suddenly remembered his boat stranded on the Sirens' shore, and Parthenope singing as he tugged. Calypso and he strolled toward the cave door, embracing awkwardly around the neck, as lovers will.

In the days before the child was born, Calypso's behavior was a revelation. Penelope in a similar plight had been most querulous and difficult; she had shattered the house with her bad temper, abused the servants, insulted him. In fact, she had more than implied that what she was going through was a curse directly consequent upon marriage with so heartless a man. It had reconciled him to the idea of having no more children. But Calypso's health was better every day, her spirits were of the brightest, she couldn't look at Odysseus without feeling grateful and giving him a colossal hug. He had never suspected that childbirth could be so easy for the husband.

Moreover, it wasn't her health she worried about, but his. Each day the table was spread with richer and more tempting foods, and when he expressed a fear of corpulence, she reminded him of the years of hardship and of the necessity of storing up a reserve while he had the chance. She insisted on a nap for him daily after lunch, and though in his heart he thought the practise effeminate, he gave in and enjoyed it.

[191]

Not an unkind word passed between them, nor an irritated thought.

He did wonder how they were to manage when the crisis arrived. In that realm he was helpless, he knew, and if anything went wrong with Calypso he'd be awfully lonely. But her cheery manner inspired confidence. He kept his hesitations to himself.

When the moment came, she amazed him by going for a long walk. For once she refused his company, and commanded him, in no uncertain tones, to keep to his end of the island. A few hours afterward she returned, carrying in her arms a small son.

Small is the word. Odysseus had never seen anything so minute in human shape. Calypso held it out to him. She was very pale. He ascribed the pallor to her recent ordeal.

"The biggest of them often start out that way, don't they?"

"Let's hope so," said Calypso. She put the infant in warm blankets on the couch, to sleep, and thoughtfully went about the preparation of supper.

For a year or so the child gave them considerable worry. There was nothing outwardly wrong with it. It had its father's love of good food, and the supply was generous; it slept regularly; it had an excellent disposition, and smiled patiently whenever its parents tried to amuse it. But it had also a certain wilted manner, like a fire imperfectly ignited. It was slow in walking and late in speaking; even after it had learned, it preferred to sit still and say nothing.

They had it out on the beach, one day, on a blanket spread over the sand. Calypso hoped sunlight might put heart into it.

"Odysseus, dear love," she said, "I wish you'd tell me more of your adventures."

"There are no more—I told you everything."

"You're a brave man, and it would be your way to conceal from me the extent of your hardships. You must have gone through terrible privations."

"Yes—I suppose I did—but they're past now."

"You often went hungry for a long time, didn't you?"

"Oh, yes, often. Among the Lotus-Eaters—I'll

never forget that bread—and that day with the Sirens."

"You didn't tell me about that," said Calypso. "Didn't you have food on the ship when you sailed by?"

"Plenty, but I lost my appetite. I'd rather not talk about it."

"If I knew," said Calypso, "perhaps I could think of a cure."

"Oh, there's no mystery about it, only the subject is unpleasant. The Sirens live on air. They're not human, you know. If any one visits them, he dies of starvation. I can see them now, one of them on the shore, one of them half-way to their house, the other between those two, sitting there in the sunlight waiting for their next victim. I could imagine the bones of the unfortunate mariners strewing the meadow."

"Could you actually see them?"

"Not from the boat, but I imagined them. In fact, there would be some recent cadavers, logically. The thought made it impossible to eat—in fact, from that moment till I came here."

"And meanwhile you went through a severe ship-wreck! That's enough to explain anything. You can't expect to be yourself for a long time after that. I'm glad you came where there was wholesome food, and your naps have built you up. Don't you think you would feel more alert if you began to take regular exercise again?"

Odysseus for the first time was on his guard. The food had appealed to him, and the naps had proved essential, but the mention of exercise suggested Circe and the sty.

"What do you want me to do?"

"Nothing for me, dear,—it's for you. There's no work here, as you know. You'll have to invent something—chop down trees, take a walk up the hill, swim—a clever man like you can think of something."

She kept at him till he took her advice. The swimming first. It palled on him. Nothing could be duller than walking up and down the hill. He took the ax and began to chop down trees, trimming them into shapely logs, and laying them in neat piles. That was something like! He began to

[195]

remember the war, and the strenuous work when the ships were building to follow Helen. What a bustling world that was! And at Troy, the walls they put up to shelter the fleet! And great Achilles, storming through the plain! Even Agamemnon— not so bad in the early years.

The toil in the hot sun browned him, and the heavy blows hardened the muscles of his back and arms. Calypso and the boy would sit near, watching. She said the play of his body was a symphony.

And the boy came along gradually, in his own way, a gentle harmless child, undersized, but healthy enough. He began to resemble his father. Calypso was a happy woman, once more care free.

When Odysseus had cut down and piled the trees off a five-acre lot, she had another frank talk with him, one evening when the boy had been put to sleep. Once more they wandered toward the cave door, with their arms around each other's necks.

The coming of the second son was really the happiest event Odysseus ever looked forward to. He had nothing to worry about now; Calypso always managed well, and the child was sure to arrive safely. She was in wonderful spirits, of course. They had pleasant debates over the name, in case it should be a girl, as Odysseus thought it would be, on the law of chance and probability, or a boy, as Calypso hoped. The first son was led to believe that a bird might come from the mainland at any moment, bringing another member of the family.

When the moment arrived, Calypso took her usual walk to the other end of the island. Odysseus was so confident, he took his usual nap. He was roused by her happy voice.

"See what we have now!"

A son, to be sure, a robust, full-sized infant, plump and rosy. Calypso was overflowing with joy. Odysseus spent the rest of the day making another crib, and to save work later he fashioned it large.

It was a tender and pathetic sight to watch the elder son caring for the new brother, the anemic boy looking after the stolid and eupeptic baby. Calypso laughed more than she talked, those first happy months, and Odysseus forgot Troy at one

[197]

end and Ithaca at the other. In between he dwelt in peace.

But the second child had no disposition to grow up. His size, however satisfactory at the beginning, was inadequate at the end of the year. His health was perfect—he simply was stationary. At the end of the second year he had grown unappreciably, but he had no desire to walk—he hadn't even learned to crawl. As for speech, he lacked the instinct for it.

Calypso used to put him out in the sunlight, too, with his brother on the sand. Odysseus and she were watching the children.

"I wish you'd tell me something of your early home life," she said. "You never mention it. You have a wife, and a son, I believe."

"Yes. My father's still living, to the best of my knowledge. Not a large family."

"Is your wife fond of children?"

"Not excessively—normal, I should think—she and Telemachus get on well enough."

"He's quite a man now, isn't he?"

"My, yes! He was born—let me see—ages ago."

Calypso was thoughtful.

"What sort of person is his mother?"

"She's a good-looking woman, medium sized, brunette."

"Energetic?"

"Very."

Another pause. It was his turn to speak.

"Do you think I'd better chop down any more trees? There's no point in stripping the island."

"No—the trees might as well stay."

"It's done me a world of good. I feel like a new man."

"Do you?" said Calypso. "I'm glad to hear it."

The third son arrived unhoped for, and its coming, for some reason, was not the occasion of joy in advance. Calypso had grown thoughtful and a bit serious. Not that the essential sweetness of her nature ever abated, nor her ready kindness, but she laughed less often, and there were moments, even at the table, when Odysseus found her preoccupied.

"There's nothing wrong, is there?" he would ask, and she would assure him that nothing was wrong.

But once, after such a question, she asked him whether he still longed to rejoin his wife. He had no recollection of having expressed such a desire.

"Of course I ought to be getting back," he said, "but as I look at it, one must obey the dictates of destiny. Heaven took from me my ship and my boat; I conclude I'm to stay ashore until adequate means of locomotion is furnished. . . . . I don't imply, of course, that in our happy association I see nothing but the fact that I'm stranded—from that point of view I could cheerfully stay here for ever. Perhaps I shall."

She wasn't enthusiastic. He couldn't help noticing it.

"If your wife needs you, as she very well may, I'd be troubled to think I was selfishly keeping you. What has happened to her since you left?"

"I haven't the faintest idea," said Odysseus, "but she has a gift for taking care of herself. Besides, Telemachus is there, I suppose."

"You know," said Calypso, "when I think of these two boys growing up into big men, and some day taking care of me, I can't believe it."

[200]

Odysseus looked at the sedentary infant and his anemic brother, and then at the Amazonian woman. He couldn't believe it, either.

The thought of leaving Calypso had hardly presented itself before, and now that she brought it up herself, he realized suddenly that she was too fine a woman to lose. She looked like an antique goddess seated there, against the black rocks of the shore, majestic and for ever maternal, yet for ever maiden too, suggesting perpetual springtimes and harvests, seeds sown and gathered, life repeating itself till the last round of time. He was so moved by her beauty that he got up and kissed her tenderly, and she smiled and kissed him back, and for the rest of the day they exchanged pretty caresses, as opportunity served. That night for the last time they wandered to the cave door arm and arm.

Next day Calypso took a long walk to the farther end of the island. Odysseus was surprised. He had no idea the child was due so soon. Perplexity kept him awake through his usual nap hour. When she came back, stately and serene, she brought

[201]

nothing with her, and Odysseus saw that the walk must have been simply for exercise.

"I'd like a word with you," she said. She led him to the nearest pile of lumber. "If I provide the tools, do you think you could build a raft?"

"Very likely—but why? What do you want with a raft?"

"I haven't a ship to send you home in, nor a boat. It will have to be a raft."

"I wouldn't think of crossing the ocean in a raft!" said Odysseus. "If you're going to turn me out, give me at least a boat!"

Reproach was in her eyes. "You believe I could send you away? That is, if I followed the yearnings of my heart? Haven't I proved that I love you? Don't I know your wife loves you less deeply than I, understands you less fully, will make you less happy? Many a night you will lie awake by her side and dream of me."

"That's highly probable," said Odysseus. "Why not leave well enough alone?"

"When I was on my walk this afternoon," said Calypso, "I had a message from the gods, warning me not to detain you. It broke my heart, but it was too clear to disobey."

"I'll stay till the next child is born—I might be of some service to you."

She shook her head. "As you remarked yesterday, we must follow the dictates of destiny. The saw is hanging up in the cave, right above the ax."

When the raft was prepared, she gave him one of her heavier gowns for a sail, and provided him with a goatskin of water and one of wine, not to speak of solid food. As he pushed off and the sail began to move the scow, he looked back from time to time at the majestic figure watching him from the shore, meditative, a little sad.

PART SIX

NAUSICAA RECEIVES

HOMER doesn't say that Nausicaa died an old maid, with a bitter heart, but he implies that the odds were against her. When Odysseus visited her father's house, she was still young and in her bloom, but even then her chance of matrimony was slight, and of romance, slighter. On her father's island the women outnumbered the men. Moreover, the local society ran to extremes; his family were royal, of course, but the rest of the population were pronouncedly bourgeois. Her lover must come from the sea, if at all, and in those days ocean travel was monopolized by pirates. If a pirate ship landed, there would be a fight, and what girl could wish defeat for her father? On the other hand, if the pirate got hurt, there would be no husband. And there was an inconvenient custom in that part of the world, if a single stranger, or two or three, came ashore with no good excuse, to cut their throats as a precaution. All the signs read celibacy for Nausicaa.

But youth reads signs its own way. The sea at last, she was positive, would somehow wash up good fortune, a handsome prince. No pirate—some one innocent, preferably shipwrecked; and though alone—one would be enough—yet disarming. She calculated the probabilities. At the end of her father's island an ugly current cut into the beach—after a storm all sorts of things were left by the tide. There some day she rather expected to pick a husband out of the water. She proved her faith by weaving linen for her trousseau. A great deal of linen, because he would be a rich prince. Besides, he was long in coming.

About this time, as we have just heard, Hermes went down to the Isle of Calypso, in the same general ocean, and told Odysseus to go home to his wife. Seven years the wandering hero had spent with the enchanting goddess, and one year before that with Circe. Odysseus was the next thing to an old man. But he was all Calypso had, and she was sorry to let him go. Anyway, that's what she told him. Very reluctantly she put him in the way of building a raft, having no better form of transportation to offer, and she provided him with food, wine and water, and when he shoved off, she invoked a favorable wind.

At this point something went wrong, through no fault of hers. The wind blew stronger than was necessary, the waves rose beyond reason, the raft went to pieces, and Odysseus considered himself for practical purposes finished. What saved him was the ugly current which washed wreckage up on Nausicaa's island. By the time he felt land under him, he had just strength enough to crawl out of the surf and fall unconscious in some olive bushes near the beach.

That night Nausicaa had a dream which she interpreted as a warning to weave no more but get the linen laundered, for her prospects would soon be at their brightest. Early in the morning she and her maidens took out the trousseau, loaded it upon a large cart, drawn by mules, and brought it to the

part of the shore she liked best. First they washed
the linen, and spread it on the grass in the sun;
then they washed the garments they happened to
have on at the moment; then they bathed themselves
in the ocean; and then as Homer says, while all was
drying, they began a game or dance, tossing a ball
from one to the other, while they sang. Their
voices were sweet, and they were remarkable to
look at, but none of them could throw straight.
First the ball went into the water, then into the
trousseau wagon, and at last into the bushes where
Odysseus lay. So wakened, he raised himself to
his knees and looked around. The cluster of girls
froze with astonishment at his matted hair, his
bruised and blackened face, his body plastered
with the leaves and the sand he had slept in. When
he raised his stiff joints and walked toward them,
they gave a shriek and started away. All except
Nausicaa. With much courage she stood her
ground.

"Lady," said Odysseus, "I landed here against
my will, and I hope the men in your family won't
misinterpret my presence. You are my idea of a

goddess, or at least of an answer to prayer. Happy are your father and your mother, and happy are your other relatives, and happiest of all is the man who persuades you to marry him. Fate meant nothing pleasant for me when the storm broke, and if you too decide to be unkind, I shall no doubt perish—but if you will save me, lady, may you have your heart's desire, a husband in a home of your own, and a contented life with him."

When Nausicaa heard these pointed allusions to her special case, she considered the matter as good as settled, not knowing that Odysseus was a great orator, and girls are much the same everywhere. Her domestic side showed itself at once; she provided him with the means of washing, and with oil for anointing his person afterward, and she improvised a garment for him out of the trousseau linen. When he had made himself presentable, she thought he was the handsomest man she had ever seen, and even the other maidens admitted he had an air about him.

"When we get to the gates of the town," she said, "we'll go ahead with the cart and you wait just long

[211]

enough for us to reach the castle. Then you can follow—straight ahead and the third turn to the right."

"Why can't we go in together?" said Odysseus.

Nausicaa blushed. "I don't want to have them all thinking about us—not yet, you understand."

"Ah yes," said he, but he didn't understand at all.

At the palace the first person he met was Nausicaa's mother, a kind woman but a good housekeeper. He was hardly started on his petition for temporary shelter when she recognized the linen he was wearing.

"You say you were wrecked here yesterday? May I ask where you got that garment?"

"Madam," said he, "I owe this costume to the thoughtful ingenuity of your daughter. As I was saying, my course lay well to the north, till the storm overtook me and my raft suddenly collapsed."

Just then Nausicaa came in with her father, Alcinous, who doted on her. She had been preparing his mind.

"Your raft?" said Alcinous.

"I made it myself," said the hero. "Calypso was

out of ships. I can't see why I didn't drown. But this maiden came to my aid, invited me up to the house, and covered me with this admirably woven fabric."

"Stranger," said the king, "my daughter was less gracious than I could wish. She ought to have brought you to us at once."

"Oh, she wanted me to come with her," said Odysseus, "but I insisted on waiting outside. You might not care to be friends, you know, and in that case an open display of good will on her part would embarrass you."

Alcinous approved of his high-mindedness, and Nausicaa admired his tact. She knew she could get on with that kind of husband.

"As a matter of fact," said Alcinous, "I'm not the unfriendly sort, not with you, anyway. If you wish to continue your travels, I'll give you a real ship, and you can go when you like. Or you can stay with us, I don't care how long."

"Three days is a visit," said Odysseus.

"It needn't be a visit," said the king. "Stay on any terms you like. I shouldn't mind having a son-in-law, if it came to that. Here's my daughter, and there's plenty of room in the palace."

Odysseus was so glad to hear about the ship that he overlooked the matrimonial emphasis.

"God keep you in this frame of mind!" he said. "I may reach home after all."

Nausicaa was so glad to hear the first part of the exclamation that she overlooked the second half, or interpreted it in her own favor.

So they fed him well, and because he was still feeling the effects of his voyage, they all retired early. In the silence of the night Nausicaa's mother lifted her head from the pillow and whispered:

"Won't it be extraordinary if it does come about!"

"What will?" said her husband.

"The marriage, of course!"

"Oh, of course," said Alcinous. "It would be a great weight off my mind."

The impression Odysseus made on them next day was progressively favorable, and they began to wonder who he was. Such qualities, as Nausicaa's mother suggested, would attract attention anywhere, and the man must be well known where he belonged.

[214]

Nausicaa thought it made no difference—it wasn't his fame she loved him for. Alcinous, however, agreed with his wife that when an affair had gone so far, you ought to know your future husband's name.

After dinner that night the blind minstrel sang of the war at Troy, of the wooden horse and of the exploits of Odysseus. He was in good voice and the song was one of his best, but Odysseus began to cry, hearing himself already immortalized in world poetry.

"We'll have no more of this," said the king. "Our guest doesn't enjoy it. The reason isn't hard to guess. He may have had a relative killed at the war, or perhaps a friend or two. ., ., . You might have had, mightn't you?"

"Well, if you want to know," said Odysseus, "I was thinking of myself. I was there."

Nausicaa clasped her hands, and a shiver of excitement went through the hall. Nausicaa's mother was calculating how old he must be.

"As a matter of fact, I am Odysseus."

Poor Nausicaa went white, her father drew back

as though some one had hit him, and her mother remembered she had disliked the man from the first. Odysseus was still wiping his eyes.

"I'll tell you my story, if you care to hear. When I left Troy on my way home———"

He didn't wait to learn whether they cared to hear. He told them how he had entered Troy, and won the love of Helen; how he had saved from the Lotus-Eaters his reluctant and impressionable crew; how Circe had tried to enchant him, and how he had successfully resisted; how he had heard the Sirens, and had been bewitched by their singing, yet had sailed by without faltering; how Calypso had detained him and had asked for his love, but the gods had very kindly sent him on his way, beyond the designing woman's power. He must have come to believe his version of the facts, he told it so well.

It was a long story, and Nausicaa couldn't keep her mind on it. In a general way she understood he had been detained on Calypso's island, but she missed the Circe episode. She got the point, of course, that he loved Penelope and no one else, and his one desire all along had been to reach home. Well, though she couldn't have him, she could admire him. Only a great husband would be capable of such singleness of affection. She was glad such a man lived, though not for her.

The recital ended at last. Most of the company were sleepy, but Odysseus was stimulated by the review of his own adventures, and didn't feel like retiring. He was among the last to leave the room. Nausicaa was leaning against the side of the broad doorway.

"When you get home to your wife," she said, "will you remember me?"

He was so pleased with himself, he would have promised anything to anybody.

"Nausicaa," he said, "if I ever reach my own country, as you suggest, I'll remember you daily, as long as I live."

Her mother comforted her, as the party went to their rooms.

"He was too old for you, anyway, and I'm not sure of his character. Of course he's famous now, but before the war there was talk about him."

[217]

"I couldn't have loved him if he hadn't been a fine man," said Nausicaa between her tears. "It's no comfort to have you run him down."

"Then we'll say no more about him," said her mother. "But I can't go through such an experience again. Think twice before you rescue another one."

Next day Alcinous gave Odysseus a good ship and said good-by.

The longer Nausicaa reflected on this episode, the deeper her gratitude that heaven had permitted her to see the man of her choice. The tide might so easily have washed up a husband fairly good but without distinction of character or mind, and she might have married and been moderately happy, and then another storm might have brought in a real hero, the one she ought to have met first. Just imagine! There would have been nothing to do about it, of course, because for people like Odysseus and her, once you're married, you're married. Wasn't it far better to meet the best man first, and have something to measure the others by? There might be no others, to be sure, or if there were, they would be inferior and she wouldn't consider them,

[218]

but the consoling principle remained; he was her
ideal, and if our ideals can't be realized, at least
it's well to have them confirmed. As she said to her
mother, the last time they argued about it, next to
the happiness of marrying a man like Odysseus was
the satisfaction of having met him. Her mother,
being irritated at the moment, said she detected
a note of imbecility in this sentiment. Alcinous
said nothing; why discuss a suitor who had gone
home?

Nausicaa put the linen away. To weave more
would have been treachery to a spiritual vision.

But after a while she began to speculate about
the character of Penelope, that remarkable wife
who could hold the loyalty of a brilliant man no
matter how long he wandered. What was the secret
of her charm? Nausicaa would have liked to imi-
tate it. Undoubtedly the woman had a good mind—
Odysseus wouldn't care for a merely affectionate
companion; and thought she was probably good-
looking, yet her appeal was of the spirit—his fine
nature would not be satisfied on a lower plane.
Nausicaa, conscious of the stagnation on her

father's island, wondered enviously how Penelope kept up with the intellectual world on still more remote Ithaca.

She made what inquiries she could, as time passed and rumor came her way; very tactfully but persistently she tried to envisage Penelope's goodness. The first ventures of her curiosity yielded only this, that Penelope was a great weaver—she was at her loom all the time. Nausicaa could make nothing of this report. If you wove all the time, what a mountain of linen you would have, and Penelope wasn't going to be married. It didn't seem necessary, just to welcome your husband.

Seven years after the visit of Odysseus, King Alcinous died and Nausicaa ruled the island with suggestions from her mother. Then her mother died and she ruled as she pleased. About the time of the king's death there was a terrific storm, and much wreckage appeared on Nausicaa's beach. It stirred her heart with memories, but as no sleeping hero was found among the debris, the incident was important only as a matter of weather. Strangers landed now, if at all, when the weather was fair. The old way of treating pirates had gradually come

back in her father's later years, when poor health
had made him nervous. After his death the custom
maintained itself by sheer momentum. When Nausicaa was on the throne, the captain of her men-at-
arms would report these casualties to her as they
occurred, and she would accept the news without
sentiment; in the philosophy she had arrived at
there could be no connection between these catas-
trophes and that one bright visitation.

Then one of her seamen returned safely from a
business venture of his own, and brought further
details about Penelope. While she was waiting for
her husband, she really had done nothing but
weave. That fact seemed preposterous, but it was
true. Furthermore, her house had been filled with
suitors, with men who wanted to marry her in case
Odysseus should be proved dead. Nausicaa thought
it rather unfair. She didn't blame Penelope, of
course; in fact, her conviction was strengthened
that Penelope was a woman of unique fascination,
with whom it was impossible to compete; but why
must all the suitors be on one island?

"Did Odysseus find those men in his house?" she
asked the sailor.

[221]

"He did indeed!"

"How did he take it?"

"Remarkably well. He killed every one of them."

Nausicaa looked at the sailor a moment.

"They were strangers, I suppose."

"No," said the man, "it is thought he recognized them all. They were old friends of the family."

Nausicaa changed the subject.

"What did you say she was doing all that weaving for?"

"I didn't say—I was careful not to. How should I know?"

"Well," said Nausicaa, "you might guess, like the rest of us. What's the use of travel if you don't interpret what you see?"

"I didn't see her at it," said the man. "She gave it up as soon as her husband returned."

"That excessive kind of weaving is done by women who expect——"

Nausicaa interrupted herself, preferring not to be autobiographical.

"Well, that's one of the explanations I heard," said the man. "Before Odysseus surprised her, she

did expect to marry one of them. He had reasons
for hurrying home. They say he got there just in
time."

"Don't repeat such malicious scandal!" said
Nausicaa. "That's the sort of gossip people spread
about their betters!"

"Well, you told me to guess," said the man.

It hurt her to learn that Penelope wasn't worthy
of him, but once she had met the idea fairly, she
found it not entirely unpleasant. His wife was like
that, and he knew it, and he still was true. What a
man! . . . She saw it all now—his haste to
return was his fine wish to save that woman from
herself, to keep clear his sense of domesticity, to
sustain the object of his idealism on the level of
his own incomparable loyalty.

She was very proud of Odysseus. This secret
trouble of his drew them together. In that brief
visit, she saw now, he had understood her; when he
had promised to think of her every day, he had
known what she was asking. Spirits so sympathetic
as theirs needed no words. Had he been free then,
she had no doubt of it, he would have married her.

[223]

How hard it must have been for him, a great prince, to suffer all the inconvenience of travel, that he might return to an uncongenial house! And how splendid of him, having looked on youth and beauty in the person of a princess who shared his ideals and would collaborate in their achievement, to return to his duty without making a sign which might be misconstrued as wavering from the strict path! Nausicaa's manners, as she went about the palace, were notably gracious, subdued but sweet.

Some seven years after her fatᵢₑr died, another severe storm beat on the island. The older inhabitants said it was one of the worst, and those who had nothing else to do examined the shore rather carefully, in hope of plunder. In the very corner of the beach where Odysseus had arrived, they discovered an unconscious young man, much bruised and shattered, in his lack of attire and otherwise suggesting parallels to the great traveler, who naturally had become a local legend. The coincidence was so obvious that they reported to Nausicaa, and asked for instructions.

Long ago she had thought herself reconciled,

but now her heart beat quickly, and she felt her face go red.

"What does he look like?"

"Quite civilized," said the captain of the guard. "Nothing about him suggests the seafaring life. We examined his hands, and he hasn't been much of a fighter, not recently. I'm bound to say he seems probably harmless. Certainly he's young."

Nausicaa remembered her own thirty-two years. She began to wonder why he hadn't come ashore in an earlier storm, but she put the thought away, as disloyal.

"I should like to see him," she said. "Give him proper garments and food, and let him rest. Later in the afternoon I'll hear his story."

She found herself nervous, and took a walk with two or three of her women, to recover poise. She chose the beach, with the surf still pounding on it, and against the protests of her attendants went as far as that fated spot where she had washed her trousseau, and where her visitors had formed the habit of arriving.

When they introduced the castaway, he was

[225]

calmer than she was. She thought Odysseus had come back, the resemblance was so strong. But this man was young, as the guard had said—not more than twenty, she judged—and he was taller than her hero, slim and panther-like, a beautiful creature but perhaps dangerous, after all. In his large soft eyes she thought she saw possibilities. She settled back in her father's throne, and tried to look adequate.

"Stranger," she said, "what are you doing on our shore?"

He shifted lazily to the other foot.

"Madam, in spite of your hospitality I'll admit I'm here against my will. Far from wishing to disturb you, I never heard of the place before. The storm wrecked my boat, and here I am."

He had the voice of Odysseus, but not his eloquence. He didn't seem to care whether he talked or not.

"You don't look innocent," said Nausicaa.

"That's because I'm tired. My mother says I always look innocent when I'm rested."

"Where are you bound for?"

[226]

"Ithaca, madam."

Nausicaa wouldn't let her face show what was going on inside of her. She waited a second or two, and breathed deep.

"Ithaca, I suppose, is your home?"

"In a sense, yes. Partly so."

"What is Ithaca like?"

"Madam, I've never been there. My mother lives on another island, a distance from here, but my father is the king of Ithaca. I'm on my way now to make his acquaintance."

Nausicaa swallowed hard.

"What's your mother's name?"

"Circe."

She had expected Calypso—she didn't place Circe.

"And your father's?"

"Well, he stayed so short a time, mother never got it accurately. She had her own way of addressing him, she says. Of course she told me the general sound, and I think I could recognize it if I heard it, but when I get there I'll just ask for the king."

[227]

In spite of herself Nausicaa admired his ease and his confidence. The boy evidently inherited his father's greatness of mind.

"The king of Ithaca," she said, "is Odysseus."

"Oh, is he? Mother didn't have it right at all."

"King Odysseus stayed here with my father, on the way home from your mother to his wife."

Circe's son seemed not impressed.

"Did your mother tell you he already had a wife at home?"

"Oh yes—and a family."

"No!" said Nausicaa.

"Yes, when he went to Troy he left a son."

"I never heard he had a family," said Nausicaa, "but of course it wouldn't be surprising—not in his own home."

"In his case, mother says, it wouldn't be surprising anywhere."

Nausicaa rose, to end the discussion.

"If your mother has such an ignoble opinion of her lover——"

"Such a what?"

"If she thinks he was so wicked——"

"Now, don't misunderstand me! Mother meant——"

"I was about to say," continued Nausicaa, "it's odd she'd want you to associate with your father."

"Perhaps she doesn't. I didn't ask her—I thought I'd better know him, because, from what she said, he must be my ideal man."

Nausicaa turned white.

"Your mother lied! He thought of only one woman, his wife! When he visited my father——"

"Didn't he make love to anybody?"

"He did not."

"Well," said the boy, "there couldn't have been anybody here."

That evening Nausicaa dined alone. The food her women brought didn't tempt her; she rested her elbows on the table, informally, and her chin on her hands. After prolonged thought, she called in the captain of her guard.

"Weren't you with my father the night Odysseus told his story?"

"In this very room, madam."

"Did he say anything about Circe?"

[229]

"Why, don't you remember? One of his best episodes."

"I must have been thinking of something else," said Nausicaa. "Who was she?"

"The fierce witch who turned his men into swine. You can't have forgotten. He found her in a palace, in a thick wood, and all her animals were playing around the gate, and inside the house they could hear her sing. She was busy weaving."

"What was she weaving for?" said Nausicaa.

"I've forgotten that—I don't believe he told."

"Well, go on, what happened?"

"Why, he said he had a happy inspiration, and avoided the spell, and at the point of the sword made her restore his men to their natural shape."

"Was that all?"

"Yes—practically all."

Nausicaa rested her chin in her hands again. The woman was a sorceress! In a sense, what she did oughtn't to count, certainly not against her victim. The enchantment had evidently worked on Odysseus, but just as evidently he hadn't known it. The perils that man had undergone!

But essentially he was what she had thought him.
If an ordinary woman had ensnared him, he would
have been inexcusable, he would have been vulgar.
Sorcery, however, against which there's no defense .

Her opinion of Circe was unpleasant. No doubt
the boy's manner, agreeable enough but impudent,
gave the most favorable version of his mother's
character. She must be one of those women of
whom people talked, though there would be no
example on her father's island—one who would
make love to a man. From what the boy said, his
mother thought a man admirable if he yielded.
And she thought women would succumb everywhere
to casual philandering! In short, a beastly mind.

As Nausicaa realized the depravity which had
betrayed the helpless Odysseus and had brought
this boy into the world, she felt pity for her visitor.
Surely, if he was now leaving his mother's influence
for his father's comradeship, the least one could
do would be to help him on his way. A few weeks
with Odysseus would improve his manners—how
courtly the hero had seemed, that night he spoke

to her by the doorway, their last words! When the boy had seen a true home, and the attitude of a father who accepts his responsibilities and provides for the spiritual needs of his family, this false, flirtatious ideal would be sloughed off.

She raised her chin from her hands.

"I'd like a word or two with that young man, if you'll bring him in."

She started toward her father's throne, but decided the table would do better. When they brought him in she had him sit down opposite her.

"I'm glad you sent for me," he said. "My room is as cheerful as a prison."

"We're not going to discuss my house. I'll simply ask you a thing or two about your mother. Is it true she turns men into beasts?"

He studied the idea.

"Mother is one of those women," he said, "who have a great deal of charm."

"That's not what I asked," said Nausicaa. "Does your mother turn men into beasts?"

"Not recently," said he. "She used to, before father met her, but she never did afterward."

"I'm not at all sure of that," said Nausicaa.

"No, I think I'm right," he said. "The gift was in the family for several generations, but it was flickering out in mother. I haven't it at all myself."

Nausicaa looked at him.

"You know the principle of it, don't you?

"Just a moment," she said. "Your mother admired your father, from her own point of view, yet she didn't want you to visit him? You are going without her permission?"

"That's easily explained. In his prime she says he was the most fascinating man she ever heard of, but she's afraid he's grown old. She says she never looks up a lover after twenty-one years."

"She doesn't know him at all!" said Nausicaa. "He's hardly beyond early middle age—the most graceful guest we've had, handsome and——"

"That may be," said the boy. "When did you see him?"

"When he was here. That's no more than—let me count—why, it's fourteen years!"

"Seven after he left us," said the boy. "And he still was well preserved? Not that it matters. I reasoned that if he was getting old, the sooner I saw him the better."

"What did your mother say to that?"

"She said, aside from his age, he wasn't the type of man that shows off well at home. She wished I might meet him somewhere else."

Nausicaa leaned her elbows on the table, in that absent-minded way of hers, and rested her chin in her hands. The boy leaned his elbows on the table, rested his chin, and gazed across at her, very friendly. She was irritated, and sat up straight. He remained in the more comfortable position.

"Why does your mother do so much weaving?"

"She does none at all."

"Your father said she was weaving when he arrived."

"She may have been, but she must have given it up. I never saw her do it."

"She doesn't sing as she weaves?"

"Not a stitch, and not a note!"

"After she caught him, those tricks weren't necessary, I suppose," said Nausicaa. "No doubt she grieved when he left her."

"I doubt it. Mother says there's a time for all things, and you shouldn't overdo your happiness. No, she was very fond of him, but his wife wanted him back, or he wanted to see what had happened to her, so he went. After all, if he'd stayed with us, he'd have grown old, and there would have been nothing to occupy him. Even before he left, she says, he was hard to entertain."

"Young man," said Nausicaa, "you had better make your father's acquaintance as soon as possible. I disapprove of your mother."

"I noticed you don't understand her," said the boy, getting off the table and sitting up straight. "You're not at all alike."

"You've noticed that, too?"

"Yes. Mother says she cared nothing about the future, and less about the past. Her best times, she says, are always in the present. So she never has to ask questions."

Nausicaa rose from her chair, slightly red in the face.

"A boat will be ready in the morning. Go as early as you like."

[235]

It took her several years to think out the implications of this visit. She continued to hate Circe, and things the boy had said, the poison of an unfamiliar philosophy, rankled. The youngster had taken life for granted, had apparently despised those who missed any of it. As she got on toward thirty-five, and then toward forty, Nausicaa felt she had missed it. That boy, with his elbows on the table, had thought of her as another piece of furniture. Odysseus would have made love, had a real woman been there! She wondered if he would have.

When she was about thirty-eight, she began to condemn herself—or that former self which had seemed admirable. Her worship of the hero never flagged, in spite of the injury Circe had wrought, but she saw life in a new mood. She hoped it was a richer fund of charity, such as time is said to provide. When she was young she had been severe toward Penelope, but now she could almost—yes, she could understand Circe's behavior. That is, she could if she cared to adopt Circe's philosophy. That is, a point of view which permitted you to enchant the man you loved, whether you ought to or not. But from that point of view, of course, you ought to. Circe had all that happiness, with the consciousness of innocence thrown in. Comparing the two philosophies, if you asked which got you further——

No, she had to admit she had worried about the future, had mourned over the past, had never once been happy in the present. Perhaps a sensitive man guessed a woman's philosophy by instinct. Perhaps, if she had had another philosophy that time Odysseus was washed up—if she hadn't asked him to wait at the gate, if she hadn't withdrawn herself while he was in the house, if she hadn't confused being maidenly with being invisible, if she only had had Circe's wisdom, to reach out to the heart that had yearned for her——

It was time for the seven years' storm, and she rather expected it, but it turned out to be mild, hardly more than a squall. No wreckage of importance came ashore. She was astonished when the captain of the guard reported another stranger.

"I'll waste no sympathy on him," she said. "Hospitality has worn me out. If he's a pirate, cut his

[237]

throat. If he's an honest man, give him food and send him off."

"You'd perhaps be interested to see him," said the captain.

"What is he like?"

"Young, madam, and good-looking in a girlish style of beauty."

"Feed him and send him away."

"Madam," said the captain, "you won't regret a word with him."

When the boy stood before her, though straight from his shipwreck, unkempt and bedraggled, she saw that he was handsome. Not very tall, not strong, but certainly exquisite. She knew also why the captain wished to bring him in. He was a pale copy of Odysseus.

It was then that Nausicaa became an old maid.

"Young man," she said, "we'll come to terms at once. Who was your mother?"

"My father," he said, "is the king of Ithaca, and——"

"Did your mother learn to pronounce his name?"

"Odysseus?"

[238]

"Correct.   And your mother's name?"

"Calypso.   She lives on an island——"

"Correct.   Do you happen to know how many children your remarkable father has, altogether?"

"He was with us seven years. I'm the eldest. My next younger brother——"

"Enough!" said Nausicaa to the guard. "Cut his throat!"

PART SEVEN

THE LAST VOYAGE

PART SEVEN

THE LAST VOYAGE

THEY say that Odysseus did not end his days in Ithaca. After he returned from Troy, killed the suitors of his supposed widow, and resumed his post as head of the house and king of the island, he found to his surprise that what he wanted was more adventure. Though no longer young, he wasn't yet so depleted as to enjoy sedentary routine. When Penelope had her mind on something else, he called his aged mariners together, one evening, got out the old boat and sailed away.

That's the story, and poets have made splendid use of it. They supplied the motives for this sudden move. Penelope bored him, they said—or he couldn't forget Calypso and Circe, the goddesses with whom he had lived, who had set a high standard—or he dreaded the futility of comfortable age, and wished to die, as we should now say, with his boots on. But they all agree that he never came back. They may have been too dazzled by the poetic implications of his end to remember that when he returned from Troy his old mariners were all lost, and his boat was long since wrecked. If he started out again, it must have been alone. Well, why not?

Plato tells another story, which at first sight contradicts the legend that Odysseus undertook a supplementary and final voyage. According to the philosopher—in one of his more fanciful and penetrating moods—a certain man, an obscure person, died temporarily and brought back to life a clear report of what he had seen in the other world. In particular he had watched the spirits choosing the career they hoped for in their next incarnation. After all the prizes had been selected, he saw a modest soul poking around for something in the pile of rejected destinies. He found it at the bottom of the pile, and went off content. This was Odysseus, and he was looking for a quiet life.

Once more, why not? He may have yearned for

quiet and still gone traveling. Or another will than his may have returned him to the restless sea.

Consider the household he came home to. Homer, of course, emphasized its sanguinary aspects—to him the important matter was the killing of the suitors and the hanging of the disloyal servants. He addressed an age which interpreted life in terms of battle and sudden death. To us the inward experiences of the soul are momentous and often quite as tragic. We are disposed to brush aside the suitors and their fate, and to dwell on the fact that Odysseus came home to a literary atmosphere. He walked right into what you might call a critical welcome. Without his knowledge the years of his wanderings had developed in several people under his roof a severe taste in story-telling. His future depended on the quality of his report.

There was Penelope, for example. Careless readers have kept alive her reputation for patience and fidelity. She fought off the suitors by pretending she was too busy to marry—she had some weaving to finish. When they wanted to know what weaving could take so long, she said she was making a shroud for her father-in-law, Laertes, and she wanted to get it just right. This is indeed the account she gave to Odysseus, to explain what she had been doing all these years. But Homer also indicates that she was in love with one of the suitors, and her husband's return interfered with the romance. She was faithful, no doubt, in fact, but the mind is hard to control, and she couldn't help admiring Amphinomus. He was unusually intelligent, and he could talk better than any other man. Homer says she felt he understood her. There you are! Odysseus excelled as a public orator, but in intimate discourse——

Then there was Laertes, the elderly gentleman for whom the shroud was weaving. His health was still good, but his fortunes were low. In his son's protracted absence he occupied himself with humble duties on the remote borders of the estate— partly because no one provided better for him, and partly because he liked to be as far as possible from the shroud. He said nothing, but he thought a great deal, and of his thoughts, more hereafter.

Then there was Telemachus, the son of Odysseus, a nice boy, with spurts of personality, but on the whole ineffectual. He resembled his grandfather. To his father's return and to the setting out again, he contributed nothing, and he could do nothing with his mother. We dismiss him as irrelevant.

Then there were two figures in the background who really weren't in the background at all, if spiritual influences are rightly measured. Eumæus, the old swineherd in whose hut Odysseus found shelter when he landed in disguise. Eumæus was born in a distant island, where his father had been king. This father, having a taste for the exotic, had procured for his child a beautiful slave, a nurse, a tall woman whose skin was of a mysterious darkness, and who spoke with an accent. She was fond of the boy, and entertained him with tales of her people, strange legends, voluptuous and romantic as herself. The child grew discontented with his comfortable lot, though in his age he looked back and remembered more good things in it than perhaps there were. He wanted to see what his nurse talked about; he was destined, he felt it in his bones, to surprises and gorgeous encounters. He was, in fact, educated beyond his years.

One day a ship arrived in the harbor, full of

[247]

foreign men whose skin was dark, and who sold richly colored rugs, and strings of beads, and rings for the ears, and similar articles of clothing. All the women came down to the shore, and his nurse brought him along. He was seven or eight years old. He watched as she tried on two of the largest earrings, and he thought how splendid she was as she put amber beads about her neck and stood very straight, to let them fall down the deep hollow of her bosom. The women of his own race looked gravely at her; they were not equipped to make such an effect.

Suddenly he noticed that she was talking to the sailors in a language he hadn't heard before. Now and then she laughed, but the talk seemed neither frivolous nor casual. As a matter of fact, the traders were from her own country. That night the ship sailed off, without making unnecessary stir, and because the nurse was very fond of the boy, she took him along, to see the world. When they sold him to Laertes, then the young king of Ithaca, he fetched quite a price.

At first Eumæus didn't understand that he was a

slave. He came so well recommended that the queen, herself hardly more than a girl, treated him as a son of the house, dressed him well, gave him the run of the island. Her husband, with the bridegroom mood still on him, protested that he had bought the boy to be her servant, but she put him off, and later on, after Eurycleia came into the family, the subject was dropped. So long as the queen lived, Eumæus was a privileged character. He was the playmate and guide of her children, as they arrived. He even had hopes of marrying her last daughter, but the girl was a little young for him, and it was really the mother in her that he admired.

Then the queen died. Odysseus met her in the lower world, on his way home. Eumæus at once became the official swineherd. The suitors didn't appreciate him, and Penelope had never liked his attitude to her mother-in-law. In his hut at night, in the fields by day, he reviewed his career, longed for the good things he had missed, and exaggerated those he had had. The imagination his nurse had stimulated, long ago, was still working.

Last, there was Eurycleia. Homer crowds her story into one of his marvelous sentences, a life in ten words. Laertes bought her a few years after he purchased Eumæus. She too was a king's daughter, she was in the bloom of her maidenhood, she too had an exotic charm, though it was of the mind rather than of the body. But after he had brought her home, the poet says, he was afraid of his wife.

Eurycleia was a modern woman. Or rather, she reacted to the dulness of a too orderly world, in the days before Helen ran off with Paris. Her generation failed to appreciate their blessings— they were looking for the tang of life. When her father got into difficulties, therefore, and she found herself exposed for sale on the auction block, she thanked heaven for a career, the only professional career, in fact, then open to women. If her father had lasted a bit longer on his throne, he would have arranged a marriage for her, but that too would have been a sale, and a less promising one. She didn't share her father's taste in husbands, and he didn't appreciate all her gifts. But in the slave market the buyers were connoisseurs, and many of

[250]

them were princes and young kings, away from home.

So Laertes found her. She saw the wonder in his eyes, the will to have her, but she saw also a noble courtesy, the reverence which goes well with a great passion. He didn't touch her, like the coarser buyers, and he didn't haggle over the enormous price. He only looked at her a long moment, and he consulted her wishes.

"I shouldn't like to bring any sorrow to you, more than fate has imposed."

He had a gentle voice. She had never been so cheerful in her life.

"You would grace a more splendid kingdom than mine—Ithaca is a quiet spot—you are beautiful enough to belong to a great hero."

She smiled, and he felt encouraged.

"The kind of person I am," he said, "I could never make your loveliness my own, if it were against your wish."

She smiled again. So he took her home, and the queen said she could help with the mending.

When Odysseus was born, they turned him over

to her charge, and she made up her mind he shouldn't be like his father. She tried to put into him courage to live. She couldn't be sure, of course, how far she succeeded—not till Troy called him, and he had a chance to prove himself. She was glad of the war. What thoughts she had, watching Laertes grow old, avoiding conversation with her, and watching Odysseus grow up, more and more inclined, she feared, toward compromise and indirection! Penelope was not the wife she would have chosen for him. He should have had a dashing creature, some one who would have encouraged, not suppressed, his initiative. But once he started for Troy, Eurycleia began to take heart. Surely something would happen to him now! He would meet people and see the world. If it was in him to catch fire, this child of her frustrate spirit, this son she ought to have borne, would kindle at last.

Well, this was what Odysseus came home to. All this ferment in the house—and he had been looking for adventure abroad.

Just before he returned, Eurycleia was talking about him to the swineherd. The old man was sitting on a stone wall, watching the pigs, and she stood looking beyond him, down the hillside toward the sea.

"It's no use," said Eumæus, "he won't come back, and if he did, it would make no difference. He was like the rest of the family, he never quite carried a thing through. His mother lacked the courage of her convictions."

"She objected to his going to the war," said Eurycleia, "but he went, you remember. I expect him back. He'll come with his ships laden, and he'll bring a captive or two. I hope he will. Those Asiatic women are lovely."

Eumæus scratched the top of his head.

"They're all right in their place. . . . Wouldn't it make a row if he did!"

"Not if he's the man I think he is! When he comes back, he'll know how to handle Penelope. That is, if she's still here."

The swineherd looked interested.

"Is she making up her mind?"

"Long ago."

"Well, what's she waiting for?"

Eurycleia shrugged her shoulders.

"The one I'm sorry for," said Eumæus, "is the old man."

"Laertes?"

"Yes. He never did any harm."

"No," she said, "I don't suppose he ever did."

"Well, there's one good thing about having no ambitions—no matter what happens, you don't feel you've missed anything. I don't like to see him working in the fields at his age, but he's better off than his wife. There was an unhappy woman for you! Every faculty, every gift, except courage. Romance within her hands—and she knew it too. A wasted life!"

"You still think she was in love with you?"

Eumæus retired within thoughts too sacred for utterance.

"If she was, I congratulate you on your escape! What a tongue she had!"

Eumæus got off the wall and started after his wandering charges. He permitted himself an irritated word or so.

"You don't understand such things. How could

you? If she had had what she wanted, her tongue wouldn't have been sharp. She stuck to the old fellow from a sense of duty. Very fine of her, but it was a strain. He never was what you'd call a man."

"I knew him in his youth," said Eurycleia.

"So did I," said the swineherd. "I knew him before you did."

He followed the pigs across the field, and she continued to gaze off at the blue waters. It was a crystal day, radiant and clear, immortal weather. She couldn't realize she had grown old. Whatever her body said, something within her still matched this sunlight, some divine eagerness which had not yet been answered. Even if Odysseus did come back a great man——

She wished she were a rich woman on an island where the hero would stop on his way home. Much she'd let him go home! How she would waken that timid heart of his, and teach him the fire and the depth of life!

Well, perhaps some woman was rendering that service. Some remote woman, in a strange sea, who would act on her impulses. Odysseus would come back a great lover. No, that wasn't the point—he would leave behind the family strain of cowardice.

Her own potential lover—her master, so to speak—was probably digging in the vineyard. He didn't hear her coming, so she had time to observe his condition. He wore a dirty cloak, much patched, and leather leggings and sleeves, to protect him from the thorns. He made heavy work of the hoe, he was so old. She wondered if in his eyes she too seemed old, or whether he maintained within him, as she did, the conviction of youth. Her love for him had ended years and years ago. She was looking at a rather worn metaphor of life refused.

"I've been thinking of your son."

Laertes straightened his back and turned to her with watery eyes.

"He's a long time coming."

"Do you want him to come?"

The old man studied her curiously.

"Why not? If he doesn't, there's no help for any of us. Would you call this fit work for me, at my age?"

"I was thinking of him," she said, "not of us. I hope he's too busy to think of us. We're not worth it."

Laertes struck a bit of sod with his hoe.

"What would he be busy about? The war's over long ago. Why doesn't he come home?"

The woman's aged lips framed a smile, not unlike that he had seen in the slave market, when he had asked her permission to buy her. But the resemblance escaped him. He had forgotten, or his eyesight was poor.

"I hope he has found what you and I never had. I hope he has lost what you gave him—his fear."

Laertes dropped his hoe, and bent over with creaking bones to pick it up.

"Fear? Of what? You're like the rest of them now—you can say what you like."

He moved over to the next vine, and began to break fresh turf.

"Am I like the rest of them? Perhaps I've been your peculiar affliction, the test of your will. You ought to have taken me."

No question but he understood what she meant. He was quick to defend himself.

"Haven't you had a comfortable life, on the whole? . . . It would have been a mistake."

"For whom?" she said. "Not for you, Laertes. You were afraid. If you hadn't been, you would have done what you thought of when you bought me. Then you wouldn't have resigned your kingdom just because your daughter-in-law wanted to be queen. And your son wouldn't have married such a wife. And he wouldn't be off getting an education at his time of life. He'd be home now."

"Would he? Well, it's a little late to discuss it."

He began to laugh, a dry, not very pleasant laugh.

"You're amused, are you?"

"When I was a young man," he said, "I overheard two old people remembering their love-affairs. It was indecent."

She left him to his hoe and his dirty cloak. Later in the afternoon Penelope sent for her. The queen was in her weaving room. When Eurycleia came in, she was holding up the completed shroud to measure the length and fullness.

"I want the house cleaned," said Penelope. "Tell

the women to get out the mops, and begin the first thing in the morning."

"It's no use cleaning the house while the suitors are here."

"They're leaving in a few days," said Penelope. "I'm going to be married."

"That's different, of course," said Eurycleia.

"Yes, I see no point in waiting longer."

"Amphinomus?"

"Yes. If I must listen to a man talk, I'll choose one who knows how. My late husband had no sense of high lights. The way he would spin out the trivial!"

"When he comes back," said Eurycleia, "you may find him more discriminating."

"He won't come."

Eurycleia was silent.

"If you intend to criticize me," said Penelope, "we'd better get through with it now. I've been a faithful widow long enough."

"You're quite right. I shan't criticize you; I hope Odysseus won't. Somebody in this house ought to develop independence, it doesn't matter who."

[259]

"I'm glad you see it," said the queen. "I was afraid——"

"Don't be."

Penelope folded up the shroud.

"Well, that's done," she said. "I thought I ought to wait a reasonable time, for the sake of appearances, but I knew if he ever traveled he'd get into trouble."

"I hope so," said Eurycleia. "I hope he's been doing what he wanted, whether it's good or bad. Just as I feel about you."

"Then you do think my wedding a mistake?"

"We'll find out as you go along, but it's really not important. You've made up your mind. That's the main thing."

Penelope looked in the mirror, and tucked away a gray hair.

"To-morrow, then, right after breakfast. I'll announce the engagement this evening."

That evening Eurycleia stole off to tell Eumæus the news. In his hut she found a strange man, a dilapidated traveler. Eumæus was trying to do the honors, and at the moment the wayfarer was

[260]

taking a bath. By the scar in his foot she recognized Odysseus.

At first she thought she wouldn't tell Penelope. Why not see what would happen? Then she decided to bring on the crisis at once. The queen was coming away from the banquet hall, where she had struck consternation into all but one of the suitors, and had made it not entirely pleasant for him. Clearly she had enjoyed herself.

"What is it now, Eurycleia?"

"Now," said Eurycleia, "it is your husband. He has returned."

Penelope took the blow amazingly well. After all, she had some great qualities. She started upstairs deliberately, then turned half-way.

"If my husband wishes to speak with me, I am in my room."

After he had met the suitors, and all that, he did wish to speak with her.

"She is in her room," said Eurycleia.

The moment was fateful. If he had really developed greatness, off the battle-field, wouldn't he tell his wife to come right down? . . . Well, he

[261]

walked straight up the stair carpet. And first he wiped his bloody sandals on the mat.

Penelope too understood the strategy of defense. She spoke first.

"Where in the name of heaven have you been?"

"At Troy," said the hero.

"That was over ten years ago."

"Yes—I've been trying to get home."

"Trying, my dear man! Who kept you back?"

"Fate."

"What was her other name?" said his wife.

"You haven't changed, have you!" said he. "Who were all those men down-stairs?"

"We won't get off the subject just yet. Where have you been staying?"

"It's a long story," he began.

"Oh no, I've guessed the gist of it. You've been——"

"The last time I told, my adventures," said Odysseus, "it took the best part of an afternoon and evening, and I left out a good deal. If you think I'm ashamed of any of it, you've guessed wrong. As soon as you've explained the goings-on

[262]

in the house, I intend to call the servants together, and give a full account of my absence. Perhaps you'd prefer to make your confession public, too."

"I've none to make. There's no parallel between your conduct and mine. If you had come home early, I shouldn't have been annoyed by those men. They thought you were dead, and they wanted to marry me. There's nothing to explain in that."

"For ten years they've been making an innocent but continuous offer of marriage?"

"It was embarrassing, but what could I do?"

"That's what I'm wondering," said her husband. "What did you do?"

"Most of the time I wove."

"Did I hear correctly?"

"I've been making a shroud for your father."

"Isn't it a bit large?"

"It had to be done over several times—and you might understand I wasn't in a hurry to get it finished."

"My father wasn't either, I dare say. How did he like your forethought?"

[263]

"Your absence has grieved him—he rarely talks. You haven't been very considerate of any of us."

"That's a matter of opinion," said Odysseus. "But my wanderings are over now, and we'll start fresh. I'm glad to see you looking so well. When we've all had a chance to rest, I'll entertain the family some evening. My adventures make quite a story."

"I think," said Penelope, "we'll hear that romance now. It will be nearer the truth than if you had more time."

So, late as it was, they went down to the great hall and had the household in. Odysseus gave his father a front seat, and the old man was appreciative but sleepy. Telemachus arranged the servants in the back of the room, till his mother told him to be quiet. Her manner of listening suggested reserve of judgment. Eumæus and Eurycleia had their own critical points of view.

"I'll skip Troy," said Odysseus, "you've heard about it."

"Tell us who was there," said Penelope. "I can imagine the rest."

[264]

"Another time, my dear. I now wish to report on my private adventures."

There was timid applause from the back of the room. Eurycleia began to be proud of him.

"As I told the king of the Phæacians——"

"King?" said Penelope. "Is that where you stopped?"

"That's one of the places. The king had a wife, but she knew her place. I did my talking to him. As I said to him, we left Troy in good order, but somewhat elated. The first island we came to, my men plundered. Against my orders, of course. At least, I told them to hurry on before the natives could rally. Unfortunately, we delayed too long."

"What sort of plunder was it?" said Penelope.

"It's immaterial now," said Odysseus. "They sank with the boats later on. Of course I held aloof from that sort of thing myself. Then we came to an island where the people lived on lotus fruit. Those of my men who tasted it forgot their homes and their wives, and desired nothing more than to rest there for ever."

Penelope looked at him sharply.

[265]

"Another time, my dear. I now wish to report on my private adventures."

There was timid applause from the back of the room. Eurycleia began to be proud of him.

"As I told the king of the Phæacians———"

"King?" said Penelope. "Is that where you stopped?"

"That's one of the places. The king had a wife, but she knew her place. I did my talking to him. As I said to him, we left Troy in good order, but somewhat elated. The first island we came to, my men plundered. Against my orders, of course. At least, I told them to hurry on before the natives could rally. Unfortunately, we delayed too long."

"What sort of plunder was it?" said Penelope.

"It's immaterial now," said Odysseus. "They sank with the boats later on. Of course I held aloof from that sort of thing myself. Then we came to an island where the people lived on lotus fruit. Those of my men who tasted it forgot their homes and their wives, and desired nothing more than to rest there for ever."

Penelope looked at him sharply.

[265]

"I didn't taste it myself," he added.

"Quite a number of things you didn't do."

Eurycleia, in the back of the room, began to look worried.

"At least I put out the Cyclops' eye. We came to him next—a giant cannibal who shut us up in a cave and ate a few of us every day."

"How did he catch you?" said Penelope.

"He didn't, really. We didn't know it was a cannibal till too late. We happened to land on his island, and took him a gift of wine and other things, just out of courtesy, and the first thing we knew, he shut the door of his cave, and there we were."

"Why didn't you come on home? Nobody expected you to pay calls all along the way!"

"You have to follow the custom of the country," said the hero. "Everybody stops at islands over there. As I was about to tell you, I put the fellow's eye out with a burned stick, and when he opened the door to let the sheep go through, we got away."

Eumæus started to laugh, but remembered his manners. Odysseus was nettled.

"But for a real adventure———"

[266]

He was on the point of telling about Circe, when he caught the expression on his wife's face.

"For a real man-sized adventure, I recommend to you a cave with a Cyclops in it and the door shut. It's nothing to laugh at!"

"Weren't there any more islands?" said Penelope.

"Several. But usually deserted. Once we came on a witch, rather distressing to look at."

Far-off memories woke in Eumæus. He forgot where he was.

"When I was a boy I heard tales about witches. They were always tall sinuous women, and they sang well. I hope the enchantress you met——"

"This one kept pigs," said Odysseus.

The room was silent. He went over in his mind his other episodes. The Sirens—Calypso—Penelope had her eye on him.

"Well, that's about all."

"That never took ten years," said Penelope. "What else have you been doing?"

"It's getting late," he said. "The other incidents are minor. The visit to the Phæacians—but I told you about that."

[267]

"You didn't—you barely mentioned them."

"And I heard the Sirens—but their singing is overpraised."

"What do they look like?"

"They were singing from a distance—I didn't stop."

"You wish me to believe you visited the pig-woman but passed the Sirens by?"

"That's about it," said Odysseus. "God strike me if I'm not telling the truth."

"Ten years!" murmured the queen. "I'd like to know where they went."

"I visited the other world," said he. "That took a lot of time. Some interesting people there. One woman in particular."

He had their attention now, and he looked Penelope squarely in the face.

"My mother, that is. I had a long talk with her, and she told me what was going on in my home."

It was a good shot, but his wife kept her poise.

"I'm not surprised she interested you. If a woman in her grave couldn't tell a better story than you've brought home, I'd blush for my sex."

[268]

Then they got Laertes to bed, and shut up the house for the night.

Of course the servants discussed the scene afterward. Eurycleia was too mortified to say much, but Eumæus rambled on interminably.

"Lotus-Eaters and one-eyed giants! Not even the beginning of a story! Why, in my father's country the children told one another better yarns than that, and stuck to facts, too. In my country the weather used to be ideal, we never heard of a hungry man, and no one was sick. If you grew old, you didn't notice it, and no one ever died. After a hundred years or so, when you became agreeably tired, you fell asleep. Why didn't he visit that sort of country? And when *we* wanted a story—why, I remember one my nurse used to repeat about a sailor who had a magic boat you didn't need oars or sail for, and every week or so, when he was so disposed, he stepped in and the boat would fly to a golden shore where the most beautiful queen in the world waited, and she didn't mind his being just a sailor, and she never asked what he'd been doing meanwhile, but she'd——"

[269]

"The Sirens weren't so bad," said Euryclea. "Do you think he told all he knew?"

"All, and several things besides. He hasn't it in him. None of the family. They're all timid."

"I fear so, yet perhaps it's only when they're at home. I'd like to know more about the pig-woman."

For a while she controlled her curiosity, but as the months passed and the household fell into its old habit, she couldn't shut her eyes to the resemblance between Laertes and his son. Or between Telemachus and his father. The three sat around all day talking, usually indoors, unless Penelope wanted to dust the room and sent them elsewhere. Yet with the evidence against her, she clung to her faith—she thought she detected at least a spark of the heroic in him, if it weren't smothered. When he tired of salt pork, for example, he didn't complain, like the boy and the old man—he'd get into a small boat, as he had done at Troy, and catch fish off shore. It wasn't much, but she thought it a good symptom. She liked to watch him, a still shadow against the sunset, and sometimes she helped him up with the boat against the rocky edge of his island. One evening he stopped to rest a moment, before climbing the steps to his house. It was the hour she had lived for.

"You are tired to-night," she said.

"The wind was against me."

"Why did you fight it?"

"Well, I wanted to get home!"

"Why?"

He didn't understand.

"Odysseus, you ought never to have come home. You should have seen the beautiful world, all the splendid men and women, the nymphs and the goddesses who live, they say, in the wide ocean. We grow old fast, and there are so many things. But nothing here."

He took a family tone.

"I owe something to Penelope. All those years——"

"She was entertaining her lovers, if you want to know, and she had to swallow her disappointment when you returned. Why did you come? When I heard your adventures, I was ashamed of you. I hoped you were hiding part of it—but then it's base to hide anything. Do you prize only your comfort?"

"You shouldn't say that about my wife unless it's strictly true. You'll make serious trouble."

She laughed.

"No trouble at all. You're not man enough."

He thought it over.

"I *did* have adventures, but what's the use of talking about them now? It wasn't a pig-woman— it was Circe. You can't guess how lovely she is. We were happy together for a year. And Calypso. Not so unique, but well enough. Seven years. You know, Eurycleia, if Penelope had been really married when I came back, it wouldn't have been so bad. I could have gone away again without saying a word."

"Why did you leave those two?"

"It was fate. I just had to come home. In both cases the same thing happened—Circe had a dream, and Calypso afterward, that the gods or whoever it is decides such things, wanted me in Ithaca. I was sorry to leave, and they both wished me to stay, but it couldn't be."

[272]

"They were tired of you," said Euryclea. "In plain words, they put you out. Good judgment, I say! They must have been very sentimental, to keep you so long."

"Now, see here——"

"No," she said, "it's my story this time, and you can listen. I don't care how well you fought, in a real crisis you haven't yet learned to be a man. I tried to teach you while you were young; now I'll give my last lesson. Is there any food left in that boat? . . . . Then get in, row away and never come back!"

He was amused.

"I'll leave well enough alone—no more voyages for me!"

"Get in!" she said. She meant it.

"What for, nurse? You aren't crazy, are you?"

"Go back to those women of yours, or find other ones, or follow a new war, or drown in the sea. Anything, so long as you aren't afraid!"

"I'll stay at home. That takes courage, too."

"Then come with me to your wife, tell her what I said of her years with the suitors, tell her of the

[273]

women you have loved, and don't let her talk back!"

"Eurycleia!"

"I thought you wouldn't. You have two other choices. Here's the first. You get in that boat and row off, as I said, or I'll tell Penelope about Circe and Calypso."

"You must be proud of yourself!" said Odysseus. "You pretend to be the friend of my childhood, for your own purposes you draw out the secrets of my heart, and then you threaten to blab!"

"It isn't very nice of me," she said, "and I shall probably not carry out that threat. You have another choice."

She pulled a small knife from the folds of her cloak, and offered it to him.

"Blood is the one thing you don't fear. Kill me!"

"Why, I'd like to know?"

"Because you are not a man."

"You're foolish! I'll never kill you, and I shan't go! Now, you listen to——"

"In that case——" she said.

When she pulled her poor cloak aside, her fingers were old and slow. He wondered why she

[274]

unveiled what Laertes had seen, long ago, in the slave market; age, he thought, should stay covered. But her hand was quick enough with the knife. When she fell, he caught her, and found the blade in her heart.

As he thought it over, it wasn't his fault, but he'd have to explain, and nothing satisfactory came to mind. Besides—what she said about him—perhaps it was true.

He carried her to the steps of his house, went silently to his boat again, pushed off from the ancestral rock, and rowed away.

THE END

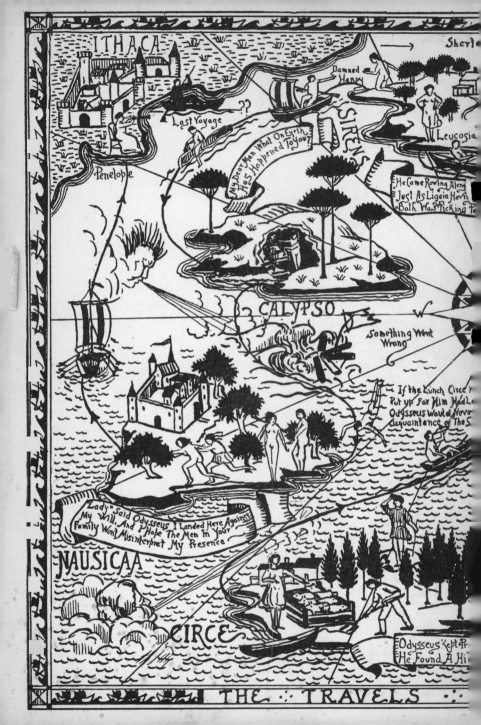